Frank Trollope

Broken Fetters

A novel. Part 1

Frank Trollope

Broken Fetters
A novel. Part 1

ISBN/EAN: 9783337045968

Printed in Europe, USA, Canada, Australia, Japan

Cover: Foto ©Andreas Hilbeck / pixelio.de

More available books at **www.hansebooks.com**

BROKEN FETTERS.

A NOVEL.

IN THREE VOLUMES.

BY

FRANK TROLLOPE,

AUTHOR OF

"An Old Man's Secret," "The Rival Doctor's," "A Right
Minded Woman," &c.

VOL. I.

London:

T. CAUTLEY NEWBY, PUBLISHER,
30, WELBECK STREET, CAVENDISH SQUARE.
1868.

CHAPTER I.

THE towers or castles dotting the banks of the Rhine are as familiar to most tourists, and, perhaps, more so, than many of the pleasantly situated villas on the banks of the Thames : we shall not, therefore, weary our readers by describing the scenery near and around the old grey tower of Lichenberg, which, rather ·more than a century ago, was the residence of one of the descendents of its ancient lords. This tower may still be seen about a mile distant from the famous castle of Rolandseck, and on the opposite bank the Old Drachenfels, so lauded by Byron. It is but little changed in appearance, since it was inhabited by one of those robber nobles who levied toll and tax upon the waters of the Rhine.

The Tower of Lichenberg, though at no time equal in size or grandeur to either Rolandseck or Drachenfels, was of considerable extent. It is not, however, our intention to carry our readers back to the period when it was in its glory—our tale is of more modern date.

This tower was assuredly neither a very commodious nor a very desirable habitation, notwithstanding the magnificence of the scenery by which it was surrounded, for it stood amid ruined walls, covered with ivy and creeping plants, broken ramparts, huge beams, and timbers rotten with age : to add to these mementos of the past, the rock, a precipitous mount, on which these ruins stood, required stout legs and good lungs to ascend, and careful steps to descend ; for neither its former nor its present possessor had taken the least pains in mending, improving, or repairing the crooked or steep path leading to its entrance.

The ruins contained, at this period, four habitable chambers—viz., a kitchen, tolerably well stocked with culinary articles, under the charge of a very old woman, who looked as grey and grim as the old place itself; a chamber over the kitchen, which served as dining, drawing, and breakfast room; and two other rooms higher up, converted into bedrooms, which were reached by a narrow circular stair.

In the dining-room, seated before a blazing log fire, on a bitter cold day in the month of December, was a young man of about twenty years of age. His well-set and well-shaped limbs were stretched out to court the cheerful blaze; his head rested on his hand, and his elbow on a table covered with books and musical instruments. He was deep in thought, looking steadily at the blazing log, and to judge from his countenance, his thoughts were none of the pleasantest.

This room was a strange looking place, and strangely furnished ; it was unlike our modern rooms—it was circular, with one very large window, filled with remarkably small diamond-shaped pieces of glass let into leaden frame .

Covering the walls was some very elaborate and curious old tapestry, and upon the tapestry hung articles of a very heterogeneous character—here a curious piece of chain armour, surmounted by a remarkable casque, belonging to one of the old chieftains of the castle, and shaped liked the beak of a huge bird; next to it was suspended the portrait of a lady, in a massive and tarnished frame; then a very antique cross-bow, over a ponderous matchlock, which at the period it was used could not have been a very formidable weapon, for in ninety-nine cases out of a hundred, the individual aimed at would have

assuredly escaped unscathed. Then came
sundry fishing-rods, ancient and modern; one
or two formidable looking horse pistols, a
couple of short carbines, a rusty spear, nets
of singular shapes, a shelf, on which were
arranged thirty or forty volumes of works of
the period, a cabinet of antique shape and
richly ornamented, a round table and five
chairs, all of venerable age, which completed
the ornaments and furniture of the chamber.

After a few uneasy turnings in his chair,
the youth, probably tired of his train of
thought, arose and went direct to the casement, which he opened, and gazed anxiously
out upon the wintry scene around. He was
tall and graceful, with every appearance of
activity combined with strength. He was
simply, though handsomely, clad in a hunting suit of dark green, the jacket braided
closely with black cord, and the collar and
edges trimmed with the fur of the squirrel.

Leaning on the window-sill, he looked
down upon the foaming waters of the Rhine,

for the wind blew heavily against the rapid stream of the river, forming mimic crests to its short waves—looking like the ocean in miniature. Two or three of those strange looking crafts which to this day navigate the waters of the Rhine, but little changed in form or rig, were ploughing their way up the stream, glorying in the gale that enabled their bluff bows to breast the current.

The Towers of Drachenfels, despite the power of the wind, were wrapt in mist. The summits of the hills lining each side of the river, forming an avenue, were covered with a recent fall of snow, and the fierce gusts as they howled around the craggy mount, on which the old tower stood, beat against the face of the youth with an icy chillness.

It was, in truth, a cheerless scene at that period of the year; and the young man, closing the casement, returned to the pleasant heat of the log fire. He had scarcely seated himself ere a heavy foot was heard ascending the stairs. The door opened, admitting a tall and stately figure, enveloped in a mantle, which was covered with snow, giving evidence of having been for some hours exposed to the fury of the storm raging without.

"Ha! my dear uncle," cried the youth, rising quickly from his chair, "I am delighted to see you. I have been looking for you up and down the river the whole morning, for I was not certain which route you would take, but excepting two heavy crafts labouring up the stream, not a boat have I seen."

"I came neither up nor down the stream, Otho," said the stranger, returning the hearty clasp of the youth's hand, casting aside his dripping mantle, and seating himself by the cheerful blaze. "You cannot think how rejoiced I am to see you so much sooner than I expected."

Divested of his mantle, the stranger presented to view a noble and princely figure. He was in an undress military habit, wearing several orders on his breast, decorations bestowed for good and valiant services in various courts.

This noble-looking man was uncle to the Count Otho de Briesbach, the name and title of the young man; he was, at this period of his very remarkable life, in his forty-fourth year, and was known throughout Europe by the name of Theodore Baron Newhoff. We have said his figure was noble; his features were good, and their expression pleasing, except when immersed in deep thought; then his brow was contracted, and a strange shade passed over his otherwise handsome countenance.

Possessed of a peculiar eloquence, throughout the whole of his eventful and extraordinary career, he carried out projects which others, with tenfold his means and advantages, would never have dreamed of achieving.

With respect to the Baron's early years, little was positively known, but it was ascertained to a certainty that he was born in the

county of La Monk, in Westphalia, and received a military education in the French
service. In Spain he was much noticed by
Cardinal Alberoni, but ever thirsting after
change of scene, or strongly imbued with the
spirit of adventure, he roamed through Italy,
England, and Holland. He had an only relative—a sister, to whom he was devotedly
attached. She accompanied him during one
of his rambles into Germany, and there her
beauty and accomplishments gained her the
hand of Count Otho de Briesbach, who, at
that period, possessed very considerable property.

After his sister's marriage, Baron Newhoff,
ever restless, travelled into Turkey, and was
not heard of for several years.

The marriage of his sister proved most unfortunate, and she became very unhappy.

The Count de Briesbach had an only
brother, who inherited from a distant relation
the title and vast estates of Hammerstein. To
please this relative, the young de Briesbach

was educated and reared as a Roman Catholic, and on succeeding to the title and estates, became very bigoted, totally estranging himself from his brother and family.

The Baron de Hammerstein married early in life, a lady of large fortune, and of the same religion as himself. Their only family consisted of two sons.

The estates of the Baron de Hammerstein were on the borders of the Rhine, nearly opposite the Castle of Drachenfels, extending several miles into the interior.

The property of the Count de Briesbach was also on the borders of the Rhine, adjoining that of his brother, and included several castles and towers of celebrity.

The Count de Briesbach had but one child, the youth introduced in the opening of this chapter.

We have intimated that the marriage of Baron Newhoff's sister was an unhappy one; deceived by a handsome person and an insinuating manner, she had married hastily.

Her brother, as was his wont, was at the time restless and dissatisfied; and anxious for his sister's future establishment, never enquired into the Count's character, satisfied by the knowledge that he bore a noble name, and had a fine property. Had he looked closer into the Count's affairs he would have discovered that his estates were heavily mortgaged, that he was a dissipated, reckless man, a gambler, and leading a vicious life.

Anxious to remove her beloved son from the evil examples of his father, the Countess de Briesbach had the boy, at the age of ten, placed in the College of Darmstadt. He had been only two years at College, when it was his misfortune to lose his beloved and amiable mother, who had been attacked by a malignant fever, and died within four and twenty hours.

The Count de Briesbach, immersed in dissipation, his fortune fast fading away, scarcely gave a thought to his son, but let him remain where his mother had placed him.

At this period Baron Newhoff unexpectedly returned to Germany. Astonished and shocked at finding his much loved sister dead, he enquired after the Count and his son. The former he learned was in Paris, sunk in vice and debauchery; the latter at the College of Darmstadt.

Disgusted and enraged with the conduct of the Count, he sought his nephew at the College. He clasped the boy to his heart, vowing through life never to desert or neglect him. He took him for a tour through Germany and Westphalia for a few months, during which time uncle and nephew became greatly attached to each other. After a few months the youth returned to College.

The Baron then commenced enquiries respecting the Count, and the fine property he once possessed; he tried to ascertain to what extent it was involved, but was unsuccessful in gaining any reliable information. His next step was to go to Paris, where he was shocked to find the once handsome and fas-

cinating Count de Briesbach stretched on a
couch, dying from a wound he had received
in a duel, the result of a quarrel in a
notorious gambling house, with an Italian
adventurer of the name of Vachero, who had
won a large sum of money from him.
Vachero had fled, no one knew whither.

The Count de Briesbach lived several
days after the arrival of the Baron, but in so
weak a state as to be totally unable to give
any accurate account of how his property
was involved. In fact his whole thoughts
and feelings centred in passionate repinings in
not having killed his adversary, who he
declared had plundered him of large sums of
money unfairly. At the last hour, a thought
of his poor boy flashed across his brain, and
he bitterly accused himself of his wickedness
and folly in having robbed him of his inheritance, and was only to be pacified by the
Baron's solemn promise of taking the youth
to his heart and never forsaking him.

Baron Newhoff returned to Germany and

commenced active investigations into the
Count's affairs; after weeks of tedious examination, he found the liabilities would swallow up all he had possessed with the excep-
tion of the little domain of Lichenberg, which
comprised the solitary old tower and as much
land surrounding it as would produce about
two hundred pounds per year.

Having paid all the debts and claims against
the estate, Baron Newhoff repaired the tower,
and furnished it as we have described, and
actually determined to live in it for some years,
and undertake the education of the young
Otho.   The result of the tuition of the eccen-
tric Baron was that at the age of eighteen the
Baron declared that there was not a man in
the Palatinate that could stand before him for
ten minutes with the small or broad sword;
he could hit a crow, flying, with his rifle;
strike a crown-piece four times out of five at
fifteen paces with a pistol, and wrestle any man
of his weight in Germany.

Otho laughed at these boastings of his kind

and warm-hearted uncle, though he assuredly excelled in all field sports and martial exercises. The young man pursued his studies with considerable ardour; he alternately read, hunted, fished, and rambled amid the glorious scenery of the Rhine. He was just twenty when his uncle received some letters, which he declared would completely change the current of their lives.

" I shall be away, my dear boy, a whole year. I can't tell you where I am going; but when I return we must quit this grim old place and mix in the world. You were born for other things beside the sports of the field, or poring over musty volumes. Amuse yourself during my absence." Without another word the Baron departed, on his mysterious journey.

Twelve months had passed when Otho received a letter, dated from Venice; it merely said—

" Look out for me on such a day." The day came, and with it, as we have seen, the Baron, to the great joy of his nephew.

CHAPTER II.

THE BARON and his nephew were seated before the cheerful blaze of the log fire, the table between them. They had just dined, and a flask or two of good old Johannissberg and a couple of antique drinking cups graced the table. The only light was that emitted from the dry logs; but there was a certain degree of comfort in the chamber, with its quaint furniture and decorations of ancient and modern arms, especially when the gale that raged without howled against the casement and roared amid the ruined walls that encircled the tower.

"I have never yet heard," said the young man, filling his uncle's cup and his own, "I have never yet heard the reason, or rather the cause, of the great dislike of the Baron de Hammerstein to my father ; and, indeed, I may say to myself. I certainly never can have offended him, for to my knowledge, I never saw him."

" To a disposition and temper like your uncle's, there was cause enough, Otho," returned the Baron; " and before I speak of our plans for the future, I will give you a brief outline of the causes of this aversion; and I am sorry to tell you I cannot say much to the credit of your poor father in my short sketch.

" There was not more than fourteen months between the ages of the two brothers ; they were both fine, handsome boys, at the age of thirteen or fourteen, but diametrically opposite in temper and habits. Your father was a bold, reckless boy; your uncle of a timid, retiring, and melancholy temperament. One day the two lads were rambling together, amid the ruins of an old castle near the mansion. Your father had climbed to the summit of a very dangerous tower in search of an owl's nest. Your uncle refused to mount after him, till, being taunted with cowardice and other reproaches of timidity and effeminacy, your uncle contrived to ascend; and when your father got him there, he swung himself down by the branch of a tree, stretching its branches close to the walls, and laughingly dared his brother to follow his example. Unfortunately, your uncle attempted to do so, but either from want of spirit or skill in catching the branch, he missed it, and fell to the ground. His shoulder was dislocated, and unskilfully set; and, in consequence, the poor boy grew up deformed. This was the first cause of offence, and your uncle never forgave your father, his deformity rankled in his heart.

" At the age of twenty-four, your uncle was visiting a distant relation at Frankfort, and there fell desperately in love with the daughter of a wealthy citizen. This girl, I have heard, was very beautiful, very wild, and very ambitious. She wished ardently to marry out of her own class, and listened eagerly to the addresses of your uncle. Unfortunately, your father came to Frankfort with the young Baron Von Konisberg, a bosom friend of his, and one of the wildest and most dissipated youths of Frankfort.

" Your father saw this citizen's daughter, and whether from a spirit of mischief, whether from love, or whether from any other motive, I cannot say, but ere a month had elapsed, he ran off with this frail fair one; and, I regret to have to relate that only a week afterwards, in crossing the Rhine, below Cologne, the ferry-boat was upset in a violent squall, and the unfortunate girl and seven other persons perished; the Count your father escaping, with two others, by the merest chance.

" The Baron de Hammerstein, two months after that sad event, succeeded to the title and large estates bequeathed to him by a

distant relative, to descend in a direct male
line.   Determined that none of his brother's
family should have a chance of inheriting this
property, he married, not more than a year
after, a young lady of birth and fortune, but
extremely plain in person and features.   He
has now two sons, both fine young men.

"Your uncle's estates and wealth have,
from parsimony and a love of accumulation,
become the largest and finest in this country.

" You see, Otho, I have entirely confined
myself to matters of fact. I have avoided such
comments or remarks, as would now be useless.   Your uncle's eldest son is, I hear, to be
united to a lady of birth and fortune, in about
ten or twelve months' time, so your chance of
the inheritance is very slight indeed."

" In truth, uncle," said Otho, laughing ;
" I never for an instant ever dreamt or
thought of such an occurrence. In fact, I do
not thirst half as much after wealth as I do
to see a little more of the world than is to be
seen from the top of this old tower."

"I intend that you should, my dear boy. I have been waiting for what I considered the proper time for you to commence your career in the world, and with your abilities I hope to see you win your way both to fame and fortune. What say you, my lad, to a military career, for a couple of years? By that time I shall have matured a project, that will, I trust, secure to you and your descendants a brilliant destiny?"

Otho looked into the animated features of the Baron with some surprise. He had studied, young as he was, his uncle's disposition and character with considerable penetration. He knew his high spirit, his love of adventure, and restless ambition. He also felt certain that he was not a man to rest satisfied with the usual career of men in his station and with his fortune, but that he aimed at achieving some destiny beyond the common. He was also aware of his high military skill and abilities as a commander; for he had perused letters to the Baron from distinguished generals and even princes, in which most liberal proposals were made to induce him to serve in their armies. Restless and dissatisfied, Baron Newhoff was ever seeking after something—he scarcely knew what—his ambition coveted ; but whatever it was he now considered himself on the high road to attain it.

The Baron had fought at the celebrated siege of Corfu, under the standard of the Saxon Count Schullemburg, a general who won immortal renown by baffling the utmost efforts of the Swedish Charles, even when in his full career of victory, and from that renowned general he had received the greatest encomiums for his skill and almost reckless courage, united with an untiring perseverance, at the same time offering him a distinguished command.

Otho, wondering what his uncle's projects might be, replied,

" No other profession would be so congenial to my feelings as a military one."

"I knew so—I knew so," replied the Baron, with evident pleasure.

"But what shall we do with the old tower, uncle? Shall it be shut up, and the lands left to the care of a bailiff?"

"No; I can manage better than that, my lad," returned the Baron. "In travelling from Venice here, I stopped for a few days at Mayence, and there met an old friend, the Count de Manheim, who, in the course of conversation, told me he had purchased your father's property on the Rhine, adjoining this, from the Jew to whom it had been mortgaged."

"How strange!" said Otho, with a sigh.

"The Count asked me," continued the uncle, not heeding his nephew's sigh, "if you would sell the property."

"What would he give for the whole—tower and land surrounding it?"

"He told me he would give six thousand pounds for it, or an annuity chargeable on the whole of the property he had purchased, of three hundred and fifty pounds."

" Is not the Count's offer a liberal one?" asked Otho.

"Yes, I think it not only liberal, but a most advantageous one; and I strongly advise your taking the annuity, for at the present moment I doubt if we could let the tower and land for more than two hundred a year.   Now, my lad, with the three hundred and fifty and a couple of hundred I can add to it—although I am not very rich, and somewhat extravagant—with five hundred and fifty pounds a year, and a little management, you may make a respectable figure in the army, and not be ashamed of your old and distinguished name, and—"

" I can do all that on three hundred and fifty, without depriving you, dear uncle, of the extra two hundred."

" My dear boy," cried the Baron, with a hearty laugh, "you know about as much of the value of money as a nun does of a husband; therefore say not another word on that point, and let me have my way. Are you satisfied with Manheim's offer?"

"Quite," said Otho; "it is extremely liberal. But there is a difficulty which I never thought of till this moment."

"What is that?"

"Why, what to do with poor old Terése."

"I have provided for her," said the Baron. "She and her husband are to remain to take care of the old tower, which the Count told me, if you accepted his offer, would be converted into a handsome hunting lodge; for he has purchased the entire range of forest extending inland to D——. He has two sons and three daughters."

"Well, uncle, now that I have no other difficulty to overcome," said Otho, "when, and under whom, am I to commence my military career?"

"You must serve as a volunteer, for such is the fashion of the times, as many of our young nobility do. I do not wish you to accept a commission, even should one be offered you, and your gallantry deserve it—and of that I make no doubt."

Otho smiled at what he deemed his uncle's enthusiasm.

"Yes, quite right, my lad," continued the Baron; "for I see by your smile you doubt my prophecy. It fortunately happens, that at this moment there is a brilliant opportunity for your first essay in arms. Unfortunate Italy is now selected as the field for the decision of a quarrel caused by a dispute in the election of a king of Poland. Emmanuel the Third, the new king of Sardinia, has joined the formidable confederacy of the Bourbon dynasty against the House of Austria. I had the advantage of a personal acquaintance with Charles Emmanuel before he came to the throne, by the singular and unfortunate caprice of his father, Victor Amadeus, who abdicated."

"Charles Emmanuel," interrupted Otho, "has sullied his reputation by his frightful ingratitude to his old father, a subject which is bruited abroad, and is the common conversation. His cruelty to his parent is in everybody's mouth."

"My dear boy," said the Baron, with a smile, " you can be no judge of the actions of kings. Emmanuel was wrong as a son, but perfectly right as a king. The old king, after his abdication, was wrong headed enough to marry his mistress, the widow of the Count di San Sebastiano, an exceedingly ambitious woman. She aimed at being a queen, and induced the ex-king, like a child longing for a bauble, to ask again for his crown. Now a king who dethrones himself only offers an allurement for neglect and ingratitude. No arm and scarcely a voice was raised in his defence, and he returned to his wife in despair."

" Perhaps," said Otho, thoughtfully, " his son had a right to retain the crown he held; but, to my mind, nothing can justify his outrageously taking his father from his bed in the dead of the night and placing him and

his wife in rigorous confinement at Rivoli.
It is now reported that the old monarch is
dead."

"He is dead," said the Baron, with a
thoughtful expression of countenance; " peace
to his ashes! He was a great and a good
man, and a brave soldier. His son promises
to rival his warlike father, and under one of
his generals, an old brother soldier of mine, I
wish you to serve."

Uncle and nephew remained till a late
hour of the night talking over their plans,
and settling the route they would take in order
to reach Turin.

In two days everything was arranged to
their satisfaction, and with some feelings of
regret, they left the old Tower and proceeded
to Frankfort, for the purpose of settling the
sale of Otho's property, and having the
requisite documents drawn up, signed, properly
attested, &c.

A fortnight was very agreeably spent in
the pleasant old town of Frankfort, after

which, being anxious to reach head quarters before the commencement of hostilities, they proceeded at once to Turin, where they arrived without adventure of any description.

CHAPTER III.

Two years have elapsed since the events re-
corded in the last chapter.   It was a fine
evening in the month of April when a horseman might be seen quietly pursuing his way
on the great public road from Turin to Novi ;
the latter named place being about two
leagues distant from the former.   The horseman was the young Count de Briesbach. Two
years' active service, under the banner of the
Sardinian king, had greatly improved the
Count, both in person and mind.

The short campaign had been a brilliant
series of victories.   Charles Emmanuel had
rapidly overrun the country of the Milanese,

and victory succeeded victory. Baron de
Newhoff had introduced his nephew to his
friend, the General; and twice during the war
the young Count had distinguished himself so
signally as even to attract the notice of the
king. Attached to a favourite regiment of
horse, at the battle of Buffalora, the cavalry
had to cross a most dangerous ford in the face
of a furious cannonade; the waters of the
Adda being at the time greatly swollen, and
the stream very rapid. The captain of the
troop and several men were killed by a cannon ball as they approached the brink of
the river.

Charles Emmanuel, mounted on his famous
white charger, and surrounded by a brilliant
staff, was stationed on a slight mound above
the river, looking on and directing the movements of the troops, the regiment, in which our
hero served as a volunteer, after the death of
their captain, hesitated to take the water,
under so tremendous a fire, and so rapid a
stream; Otho, seeing them turn their horses'

heads, rode boldly in front, and, carried away
by his enthusiasm and spirit, waved his sword
over his head, and, spurring his noble charger,
dashed into the stream, calling upon his comrades to follow him. Already a favourite, the
soldiers cheered, and, to a man, plunged into
the river, amid a rattling shower of balls,
gallantly crossed the stream, formed, charged
the battery that was defending the ford, and
drove the men from their guns.

"Let me know the name of the man who
led the Ninth Regiment of Dragoons across
the ford," said the king to one of his officers.

An aide-de-camp at that moment riding up,
whispered something to one of the officers
attending upon the king, who, immediately
approaching his Majesty, said,

"The Ninth Regiment, your Majesty, was
led across the Adda by the young Count de
Briesbach, a volunteer in that regiment."

"Ha! indeed," exclaimed the king. "The
same youth who so gallantly recovered the
colours at Novara;" and taking his ivory

tablets, the warlike monarch wrote down the name of Otho de Briesbach.

The following day, General D—— presented Otho to the Sardinian monarch, who not only received him graciously, but complimented him very highly, and presented him with a captain's commission in the regiment he had served in from the commencement of the campaign.

During the remainder of the war, the Count de Briesbach distinguished himself on several occasions, and at its termination accompanied his regiment to their station at Turin. There he received letters from his uncle, who had gone on one of his rambles, immediately after introducing Otho to General D——. His uncle briefly informed him that his projects were nearly perfected, and that shortly he should be ready to commence active operations.

" I have heard of you, Otho," he wrote, " and of your gallantry, as well as of your accepting a commission from the Sardinian king.

When I first wished you to serve as a volunteer, I did not think it would answer our
plans for you to bind yourself to the service
of Charles Emmanuel ; but before we parted,
I altered my views on that subject, and I rejoice at your success.   Give the enclosed note
to General D——.   It will, at once, procure
you leave of absence for one year.   Leave
Turin immediately, and meet me in Genoa at
the latest by the first of May."

Otho was perplexed to know what mighty
plans were filling his uncle's brain ; nevertheless, he set about carrying out his
wishes, for he was most devotedly attached to
the Baron.   Accordingly, having presented
the enclosed letter, and peace having been
proclaimed, he obtained the required leave,
and, mounting a very favourite horse, and
well-armed, but without an attendant, left
Turin, and took the road to Novi, intending to
cross the Bochetta to Genoa.

It was near the end of April.   Otho de
Bricsbach rode slowly and leisurely along,

for he had but six miles to travel. The evening was delightful, and the scenery on each
side of him picturesque, and at times magnificent. Halting his steed, on gaining the
summit of a hill, he turned round to look at
the lovely valley he had crossed, through
which ran the sparkling waters of a rapid
river.

A horseman was approaching from a bye
road; Otho paid little attention to him at first,
till a fine, bold voice, singing a merry hunting song, caused him again to look at the gay
rider, who came rapidly nearer, still chanting
his song. When quite close to the Count, he
ceased singing, and stopped his horse—a fine
spirited animal.

"A splendid evening, signor," he said,
civilly, "and this view is a glorious one. Are
you for Novi? my way lies thither, and you
look like a pleasant companion for an hour's
ride. I hate being alone—no doubt you
heard me singing;—I always sing or whistle
when I have no companion: it beguiles the

way, cheers your horse, and prevents your thoughts rambling upon unpleasant subjects.''

Otho de Briesbach looked with some surprise at his probable companion as far as Novi, and smiled at the easy, cool manner in which the stranger introduced himself. He was a man about eight-and-twenty years of age, middle height, muscular, and strongly built ; his features were very handsome, but a reckless wild look about the eyes gave a fierce expression to the countenance; his dark moustache and black, bushy whiskers were completely at variance with his bland tone and careless manner. He was dressed in a plain riding suit of dark brown, with high, horseman's boots. He appeared to be unarmed, and his saddle was without the usual appendages—pistol holsters—of travellers of that day.

Having scanned the appearance and dress of the stranger, the Count replied,

" Yes, it is a fine evening, but very little

left of it," and putting spurs to his horse was off at a brisk pace. .

"I know the road well," said the stranger, keeping pace with the Count; "and if, as I imagine, you are not well acquainted with this part of the country, I will serve as your guide as far as I am going. A mile from this you will come upon the six great cross roads, and they might readily puzzle anyone unacquainted with the situation of Novi. Do you come from Turin, signor?"

"Yes."

"Did you pass a travelling carriage, or rather did one pass you, with four horses, two outriders, and four armed attendants, with two ladies inside and two on the seat behind."

"No such vehicle has passed me," said the Count. "Pray what is the name of that forest to our right? It appears a very thick and extensive one."

"It is the forest of Lemino, and is more than fifteen miles in extent. It is a noble chase, and belongs to the Duke," replied the stranger.

In a few minutes they were abreast of the wood, when suddenly, from a close cluster of evergreens, bordering the road, five men, in tattered and soiled uniforms of white, and armed with short carbines, made a rush at the bridle reins of the two horsemen. The Count's horse reared wildly, and spun round on his hinder legs, thus avoiding being seized; but the traveller's, a chestnut horse, which stood its ground without starting, was held fast by one of the men, while another endeavoured to pull its rider off its back.

" Hell and furies ! how is this," roared the stranger, pulling a pistol from his vest, and firing full in the face of the man who tugged at his legs. The next instant he was un-horsed, and was thrown to the ground, while the man he had wounded, with a savage oath, raised his carbine to his shoulder to shoot him.

At that critical moment, the Count spurred

his horse amid the group, after receiving the fire of two carbines, the ball of one knocking his hat off, and the other inflicting a trifling wound on his left shoulder. Just at the moment the stranger's destiny was on the point of being decided, the Count fired, and shot the ruffian dead. Nevertheless, though the stranger sprung to his feet with an oath, a blow from the butt of a carbine felled him to the earth again. Otho, with his other pistol in his hand, dashed at the remaining three. They had no time to re-load, but they resolutely stood their ground, ready to strike with their carbines, when the tramp of horses and the cracking of whips announced an approaching carriage. The robbers immediately turned and fled into the wood. The Count rode after them, but not liking to shoot the villain nearest him, seized the fellow by the collar, and, possessed of great strength, in spite of the ruffian's curses and struggles, lifted him fairly over the pommel of his saddle, and held him there. Turning his horse's head, he rode back to where he had left the stranger.

The road was no longer solitary; a handsome travelling berlin, with four smoking horses and two postillions, had halted upon the spot. There were several attendants, two of whom were lifting the dead bodies of the robbers from the middle of the road ; another was assisting the stranger to bind a handkerchief across his head, which was bleeding profusely.

In the carriage sat two ladies ; they were leaning over the door apparently enquiring about the stranger's hurts. They turned round as the Count rode up, holding the baffled robber, firmly on his saddle. The light was fast fading, but the Count could just perceive that the inmates of the carriage were of rank, from the richness and elegance of their travelling dresses. One appeared much older than the other, who he fancied, from the rapid glance he had of her features, was a young and beautiful girl.

" Good heavens !" exclaimed the elder of
the ladies, " he has taken one of the robbers,"
and calling to her attendants she desired them
to help the gentleman to secure the miscreant
and prevent his doing any further mischief.
The Count having got rid of his burden, approached the carriage door. Saluting the
ladies, he said—

"To your timely arrival we owe our
safety."

" You are very modest, signor," replied
the elder lady, looking with surprise into the
youthful and very handsome face of the
Count; "after having killed two of those
marauders and capturing a third, you wish
to give us the merit, when in truth, but for
your gallantry, and being half-an-hour before
us, we should undoubtedly have been
attacked."

" You are too well attended, signora," replied the Count, fixing his gaze for an instant
upon one of the loveliest faces he had ever
seen. The face was that of the girl whom

he supposed to be the daughter of the elder lady.

"Ha! we are very formidable to look at," said the elder lady with a smile, "but my attendants would, I fear, be terrified at the report of their own fire-arms. Your friend appears badly wounded. If your road lies in the direction of Novi, we shall be happy to give him a seat thither in our carriage."

"I should rather have supposed him to be a friend of yours, signora," replied Otho. "I only met him on the road about a mile hence, and he made many enquiries concerning you, for by the description he gave, I perceive you are the party he spoke of."

"Indeed!" said the lady, with a look of surprise, "it must be a mistake. I saw the signor's countenance as my attendants lifted him from the road ; but he is quite unknown to us."

"I will see how he is, madame," said the Count, "and bear him your kind offer."

Otho de Briesbach dismounted, and giving

his horse to one of the attendants to hold, approached the stranger, who was sitting on a green bank talking to one of the ladies' attendants.

"I trust you are not much hurt," said the Count.

"You are a fine fellow, and a gallant one, too, by my soul," said the stranger, holding out his hand, "I owe you my life, for by the mass! if you hadn't shot the rascal in the nick of time, I might be now where many a better man has gone."

"Those ladies beg me to say you are welcome to the use of a seat in their carriage to Novi, if you feel too much hurt to keep your saddle."

"Many thanks to the ladies," said the stranger, muttering something to himself; "will you kindly say I feel well enough to ride the three or four miles I have to go? especially if you, signor, will keep me company so far. The hurt is a mere nothing. I was stunned and felt dizzy, but it is passing off."

"I will most certainly keep you company as far as Novi," replied the Count, "and will tell the ladies to pursue their way."

A loud shout and the report of a pistol caused the Count to hurry towards the carriage. It was, however, caused by the robber, who, profiting by the carelessness of the attendants, had effected his escape, one of the men firing his pistol at him without effect.

"Well, perhaps it is better that he has escaped," said the elder lady to the Count as he came up to the door of the carriage; "you would have had a considerable amount of trouble if you had taken him before the authorities at Novi ; but how is your travelling companion?"

"He feels well enough, madame, to sit his saddle, and returns you his thanks for your obliging offer. We will not longer detain you."

"Well, farewell for the present, signor; we may meet again at Novi. I stop at the Aquila Nera, and if you enquire for the

Countess de Sera, I shall be most happy to renew our short acquaintance."

The Count bowed, highly pleased, and expressed his thanks. The Countess requested his name, and he gave it.

" It is singular," said the Countess, showing pleasure on hearing his name, " that this very morning I was speaking of you. For the present, farewell ; but remember, you must be my guest at supper."

The order being given to drive on, the postillions cracked their whips, and in a minute the cavalcade were on their way to Novi.

CHAPTER IV.

OTHO DE BRIESBACH, musing upon the last words of the Countess, rejoined the stranger, who was tightening the girth of his horse.

"I am glad to see you so much better," said the Count; "do you think you are well enough to ride slowly on?"

"Yes," said the stranger. "I have quite recovered from the dizziness in my head, though, by the mass! the ruffian had a heavy hand. What were the rascals, signor? They wore a uniform I never remember to have seen."

"They were evidently either deserters or escaped prisoners. Austrians, no doubt. The

Milanese is infested with roving bands of these marauders, since the termination of the late war."

The travellers mounted, and were proceeding at an easy pace towards Novi, when the stranger suddenly remarked—

" You have served in the late war in the Milanese, I should imagine, judging by your horsemanship and skill with the pistol. By my faith ! it was nice practice when you shot that ruffian ; we were struggling together, and it required a keen eye and a steady hand to make sure of hitting the right mark."

" There was no time for deliberation," said De Briesbach, laughing, " another moment would have left it out of your power to know whose was the bullet that deprived you of life. We must inform the authorities at Novi, for those bodies must not lie exposed on the high road."

" Corpo de Bacco, signor," exclaimed the stranger, " leave the carrion to be buried by their comrades. If you mention the subject to the sbirri at Novi, ten to one but they will detain you, and cause investigations. As to myself, I am pressed for time, and must leave you just before you enter the town. My road lies to the left for a league further.

" Nevertheless," said the Count, " I cannot leave the bodies of Christians, though they be robbers, without interment."

The stranger remained silent for some time; he had lost much of the vivacity of manner evinced on their first meeting. Otho imagined he was suffering from his wound. They had arrived close to the town, whose lights were twinkling in the darkness of the rapidly approaching night. The stranger pulled up his horse, where a narrow bridle road led away to the left of the town.

" I must bid you farewell, signor, and believe me, though I may never have the opportunity of showing it, I feel deep gratitude for the preservation of my life. I should not like to have lost it, though, by my conscience, it would have been better for my soul had I been killed some six years back. However, farewell," and he held out his hand.

Otho thought his words strange, but frankly shook the hand offered.

The stranger hesitated a moment as he was turning away, and then said,

"Signor, say to the Countess de Sera that she will find the road by Alessandria and Aqui to Genoa much safer than the passage of the Bochetta. *Addio*," and, touching his spirited horse with the spur, he disappeared in the turnings of the narrow path he had selected.

"What on earth can the man mean?" thought the Count; " take him all in all, he is a strange compound—I fear a very doubt-ful character—most probably an adventurer. However, it matters not; we shall, probably, never meet again." His soliloquy was inter-rupted by his arrival at the gate of the town.

Novi was at that period a walled town, with gates, and had a small detachment of soldiers in barracks, together with a consider-

able number of *gens d' armes*, who patrolled
the passages of the mountains to Genoa,
which were the resort of bandits and outlaws,
as well as gangs of galley slaves from Genoa
and Savona.

At the gate, the count was questioned by
the *gens d' armes* stationed there, concerning
the affray he had been engaged in. Having
given the particulars and left his name, he
inquired for the Aquila Nera. By the directions he received, he was not long in arriving
there, and, having seen to the comfort of his
horse, he entered the inn, and inquired if the
Countess de Sera had arrived, and after receiving an affirmative, he was shown into a comfortable room, and the waiter deposited his
valise on a chair. This valise was the only
luggage he carried, strapped on the back of
his saddle, his heavy packages having been
forwarded to Genoa by the carrier that passed
weekly between Turin and that city.

Our hero had just finished a very hasty
toilet, washed the wound he had received

in the shoulder, and applied a slight bandage,
when the waiter knocked at his door, and entering the room, with a very low bow, informed him that the Countess de Sera expected
his lordship at supper, which was then being
placed on the table. Otho de Briesbach followed the man, and was ushered into the
saloon occupied by the Countess. A bright
log fire blazed upon the hearth, giving the
room a cheerful appearance, and a tolerably-
sized table, on which were several wax lights
and the edibles, was drawn close to the fire,
for, although it was April, Novi was a cold
place.

The Countess de Sera rose from her seat
and very kindly offered her hand to her
visitor, saying,

"I cannot treat you as a mere chance
acquaintance; I will tell you why, by and
bye. In the meantime let me introduce you
to my fair young friend, and *protegée* for the
time being, the lady Vannina de Matrà."

Otho respectfully saluted the lady, as was

then the custom in Italy, and the lady returned the salutation with considerable timidity, looking up as she did so, and the Count thought he had never before beheld so beautiful a face. They sat down to supper, but as they were all tolerably hungry, there was more eating than talking, and what little of the latter there was, consisted in mere common-place observations and civilities. We must, however, confess that Otho de Briesbach's eyes were frequently turned from the delicacies before him, to gaze on the lovely countenance of Vannina de Matrà, and when this said fair damsel occasionally looked up, which of course she did, the colour on her cheeks deepened considerably on finding the dark intellectual eyes of the young Count fixed upon her.

The supper ended, the dishes, &c., were replaced by a dessert and some good light wines, and the servants withdrew; then the Countess commenced a conversation by saying,

" You must have thought me very forgetful, and not very polite in not including your wounded companion in my invitation; but the fact is, you must be aware that acquaintances of the road are rarely renewed."

Otho smiled.

"I see by your smile that you misunderstand me. I do not consider you a casual acquaintance, for on hearing your name I felt as if we had known each other before, as I shall explain. One of my attendants informed me that you arrived here alone, so I imagined your travelling companion had left you. Was he much hurt? From some strange expressions he made use of when my servants lifted him from the road, I should imagine he is rather a strange character. What became of him?"

"I quite agree with you in thinking him a curious compound. In what class in life to place him I can scarcely imagine. Our acquaintance was very brief. We parted just before I entered the town. By the bye,

Countess, he gave me a message to deliver to you."

" To me ?"

" Yes, the message was for you, though it puzzled me. He said, 'You may tell the Countess de Sera that she will find the road to Genoa by Alessandria and Aqui much safer than that by the Bochetta.'"

" Ha !" said Vannina de Matrà; " that is precisely what you were told at Turin." And the sweet silvery tones of the girl's voice was music to the Count's ear.

" It is too late, my love, to profit by the good advice now," said the Countess. " My friends at Turin advised me to avoid the Bochetta. I positively believe our sex are fond of acting by the rule of contradiction. If they had said go by the Bochetta, as the road by Alessandria and Aqui is dangerous, I have no doubt in the world I should have gone by the latter. I daresay the signor who sent me that message, knows the dangers of

the road well, and it was very kind of
him."

" But surely," said Vannina, turning to the
Count, " there can be little danger to be appre-
hended from banditti, with our six armed attendants, and the ten *gens d'armes* you desired
the landlord to speak to the authorities about."

" And if the Count accompanies us," interrupted the Countess, laughing, " as you said
awhile ago, you would have no fear if fifty
brigands were to attack us."

Vannina blushed to the very eyes, looking
so exceedingly lovely, that we feel certain
our hero would have thought nothing of
that number.

" I am sure," he said, looking very much
pleased, " nothing would give me greater
pleasure than being permitted to accompany
you across the mountain, as far as the last
post, where I understand all danger ceases—
if, indeed, there be danger, which I should
think would scarcely be the case, where the
party is well armed. I can understand its

being dangerous to individuals or travellers going unarmed."

"There you are in error," said the Countess, rather seriously. "I am told there is a band, under a very desperate chief, that numbers more than fifty ruffians. I know that last winter there was no such thing as passing the Bochetta without an escort of dragoons."

A knock at the saloon door interrupted the conversation. The landlord made his appearance.

"I fear your ladyship will be disappointed," said the host. "I have applied to Captain Certa, in your ladyship's name, and he regrets that he cannot spare you more than four of his men, as the English milor who passed this morning engaged ten, and these will not return till to-morrow. He desired me to say, he thinks you need be under no apprehension whatever, as you will be sure to meet them on the road. At all events, he considers that your own attendants and four dragoons, all well armed, will be ample protection. Besides, he thinks the banditti have dispersed, as they have not been seen or heard of on the road for weeks."

" I am much obliged," said the Countess ; " four must do ; this gentleman rides with us. Let us have the horses early."

" Name your own hour, and they shall be ready."

" Suppose we say seven o'clock; will that hour suit you, Count de Briesbach?

" Quite, Countess."

" Then, have everything ready at seven, landlord, and let the *gens d'armes* know the time, and on no account forget to give them the stirrup cup before starting."

The worthy host of the Black Eagle smiled, bowed, and departed.

" I am afraid, Count, you scarcely relish our light wines after your famous Rhine vintage."

" They are very little regretted by me," said de Briesbach. " You promised to inform me how you—"

"Well," interrupted the Countess, who was a very fascinating, and still remarkably handsome woman, though, perhaps approaching her fortieth year, "I know what you are about to request; I see you men, after all, are just as curious as we ladies," she added, smiling. "However, a very few words will explain. General D——'s wife is my first cousin, and as you were placed under the care and eye of the General during your first campaign, you attended, with your brother officers, the balls given by my cousin, who, you know, is a very gay woman.'

"Oh! I see it all now," said the Count, smiling. "The General's lady, when the war commenced, went to stay with the Lady Abbess of the convent of St. Ursula, which is on the banks of the Po, just at the foot of the hill on which stands the Superga."

"Very true," interrupted the Countess; "in that same convent are my two daughters."

"Indeed," said Otho.

"Yes, and it is from that same convent

I have just taken this young lady, for the purpose of resigning her to the care of her guardian, the Count de Rivalora, who resides a few miles from Genoa."

"Then I dare say," said Vannina, looking at the Count for a moment, "you are the officer who saved our convent from being attacked and pillaged, and probably burnt. A dreadful fright we all had; the old nuns wringing their hands, and running wildly about, imploring every saint in the calendar by turns. Oh! I assure you we were in a sad way, notwithstanding the General's lady did everything she could to cheer us. It was not of the Austrians we were afraid, but a band of desperate and lawless wretches, deserters, and I know not what, who, we had intelligence, were advancing to pillage the place. While we were all in a state of despair—for the marauders had surrounded the convent, and would have forced the gates in a very short time,—a troop of horse came to our relief, and swam the river in spite of its swollen waters. How little I thought," continued the fair Vannina, blushing, and letting her long silken lashes conceal her eyes from the admiring gaze of the Count, "how little I thought—for I was gazing out anxiously from the top of a turret, when I saw the officer who led his gallant troop into the flood, and after gaining the bank, charge furiously into the midst of the marauders, who soon fled— that I should ever see our deliverer again. I assure you, Count, you had all our prayers that night, old and young."

"No doubt of that, my child," said the Countess, smiling; "and 1 also have no doubt that both old and young would very willingly have received the Count into the convent to thank him personally for his bravery ; but I heard from the General's lady that no sooner had the officer dispersed the gang of mis-creants, than, in the most ungallant manner, he turned his back upon the convent, and, of course, upon the old nuns and young ladies who prayed for him so earnestly that night."

" Upon my honour, Countess, it was with the greatest reluctance I did so, little aware at the time of the treasures the convent contained."

" Do you mean the old nuns, or the young ladies?" demanded the Countess; " for there is no accounting for taste at times."

" If your ladyship's daughters," said Otho, bowing to the Countess, " bore any resemblance to their mother, they and the Lady Vannina de Matrà were attractions for a poor soldier, who besides, to tell the truth, at that time was very hungry and cruelly thirsty, for, if the Lady Vannina remembers, the day was frightfully hot, though the plunge into the river helped to cool us a little, but we had tasted no food that day, and our orders were to return without the loss of a moment, as a general engagement was expected that same afternoon with the main body of the Austrian army."

" Well, Count, by that gallant action you gained the hearts of half the beauties of

Turin," said the Countess; "and," she continued, laughingly, "turned the heads of the other half. Just before I was leaving that city, I heard my cousin speak most highly of your gallantry in several other actions. You may, therefore, easily imagine my surprise and pleasure, when you told me your name; I thought of my daughters in the convent, and resolved to cultivate so agreeable an acquaintance as chance had thus thrown in my way."

The Count bowed and was greatly pleased. It was getting late, and the trio separated, mutually pleased with each other. The Count, if not actually in love with Vannina, was on the direct road to become so.

The next morning they were to depart from Novi precisely at seven o'clock.

CHAPTER V.

In the town of Leghorn there is, or there was, an hotel called the " Tuscan Arms." On the 26th of April, 17—, in a large room, or saloon, of the said hotel, were two men, both remarkable looking personages, seated at a table—on which a large map was spread—in earnest conversation. The window of the saloon looked out over the two piers that form the harbour of Leghorn and on the deep blue sea so eulogised by poets.

One of the individuals we need not describe, for our readers are already acquainted with his person and features; it was Theodore, Baron Newhoff; the other, a man of about

five-and-forty years of age, scarcely above the
middle height, but of a most extraordinary
breadth of shoulder and chest, his arms were
long and muscular, and his limbs the limbs of
a giant; to those immense proportions were
added a very small round head, covered with
a thick curly crop of black hair, with not a
particle of grey, intensely dark eyes, possessing
a restless, wild, enthusiastic brilliancy; thick
moustachios and whiskers and a small pointed
beard, all without the slighest mixture of
grey. Such was the face and figure of Luigi
Gaffieri, the then famous leader and chief of
the Corsican Insurgents, for the whole Island
of Corsica had risen in revolt against the
cruelties and tyranny of the Genoese.

Gaffieri's attire was almost as remarkable
as his figure and appearance; the upper part
of his person was cased in a thick doublet of
leather, very much soiled; his breast was
covered with a very indifferently polished
cuirass, a piece of armour out of use at that
time, except in certain cavalry regiments;

Corsica never maintained a mounted force, for the very best of reasons, their utter uselessness in a country, even at that period, without roads and intersected by continual mountain ranges and almost impervious thickets. His legs were cased in thick untanned leather gaiters, which reached above the knee, and round his waist a broad leather belt, evidently intended to contain pistols and pogniards, a large mask of dark brown cloth and a very broad slouched beaver, without feather, lay upon a chair beside him. He had arrived that morning from Corsica.

The contrast between these men, each remarkable in their appearance, was great. The tall and commanding figure of the Baron de Newhoff, attired in the rich undress of a celebrated cavalry regiment to which he had formerly belonged, his studied attention to every portion of his attire, was most marked, when contrasted with the rough and almost grotesque uniform of the high spirited and valiant Chief of the Corsican patriots.

Luigi Graffieri, though not of the highest rank in the island, possessed very extensive influence. His hatred to the Republic of Genoa was not merely great, but, in truth, amounted almost to fanaticism. But he had a kind heart, and a steady, undaunted resolution. As we remarked, when introducing these two men to the notice of our readers, they were engaged in earnest conversation. In reply to some remark of the Corsican Chief, Baron de Newhoff said,

"Then there is no doubt this time, that the people are unanimous in their determination to resist to the death the exactions of the Genoese Republic?"

"Not the slightest doubt—there never was ; but," added the Chief in a bitter tone, "it is not amongst the people, but those who ought to be an example to the people, that dissensions and diversity of opinion prevail."

"What gave rise to the present bold attempt to regain your freedom?" demanded the Baron ; "the three other insurrections

were so speedily put down, that I despaired
of ever seeing anything like a formidable
opposition to the power of your enemies."

"A spark will create a flame," said the
Corsican, "oftentimes of greater consequence
than the firing of a town in a dozen places;
and a mere spark has this time, thanks be to
God! lit a fire that can only be quenched in
the blood of our bitterest enemies."

"It seems," continued the Chief, less vehe-
mently, "that a Genoese collector demanded
of a very poor woman the sum of one
paola; she, however, had it not, small as the
sum was. The collector not only abused the
poor old dame, but swore he would seize the
furniture. She begged him to wait a few
days; but vain were all her entreaties. The
old woman's lamentations brought a number
of persons to her house, and they all took
part against the collector, who vowed he
would have them all punished with the
utmost severity. These threats enraged the

villagers, who drove him from the house, and pelted him with stones.

"A troop was sent to support the collector, and my countrymen assembled in great numbers; the tumult increased, and in an incredible short time the whole island was in commotion. A sudden and simultaneous attack was made upon Porto Vecchia, which was taken without resistance, and they would have captured the Castle of Corte, if they had had leaders. However, the rising had become so formidable, that the principal chiefs met to consult and elect leaders to follow up the insurrection.

"I had the honour of being appointed, with the Signor Andrea Ceccaldi, one of our most distinguished noblemen. Not to weary you, I will, as briefly as possible, state how we succeeded. As long as we had only the *maladetta* Genoese to fight against, we cut them to pieces everywhere. The Republic, finding their soldiers unable to hold their

positions, asked assistance from the Emperor
Charles VI., and to our vexation he sent a
body of men, under the command of General
Watchtendonk ; but thanks to Heaven,
though they killed and wounded some ten or
twelve thousand of our brave comrades, we
beat them, and held our own; but only for a
time, for the Emperor, enraged at our success,
sent Prince Wirtemberg in command of a
large body of German troops, against which
we were unable longer to contend. We,
therefore, agreed to lay down our arms on
certain conditions.

" Prince Wirtemberg was a brave and
gallant soldier, and behaved well to us. For
a time the conditions agreed upon were properly observed, but ere long the Genoese, with
their accustomed faithlessness, broke them.
We rose again, and soon regained all we had
given up, and we have now the most sanguine
hopes of crushing, for ever, the power of the
Genoese in Corsica. All we want is union
among ourselves, and that, unfortunately, we

have not. Do you, Baron, perform your part,
and bring us friends, arms and ammunition,
which you have declared to our chiefs you
have the power to do.   The moment you
land, you will be elected our King by the
unanimous voice, not only of our nobility
and our chiefs, but by the whole population
of Corsica."

"What I have offered and promised, shall
be forthcoming, and more.   I have been promised assistance from three crowned heads,"
replied the Baron, calmly.   "But you were
saying, Signor Gaffieri, there was dissension,
or at least difference of opinion, amongst your
leaders."

"Not amongst our leaders, thank Heaven,"
said the Corsican;   "but one of our most
powerful and influential families, whose vassals
are very numerous, and connections spread
nearly over the island, sides with the
Genoese."

"His name," demanded De Newhoff.

"Count Luigi de Matrà," replied the Cor-

sican, " one of the haughtiest, proudest, and
most passionate and intemperate noblemen on
the island.   He has but one child, a daughter,
heiress to his great wealth, and who, it is
understood, is betrothed to the son of the
fiercest and most inveterate noble of Genoa.
He was our governor when the treaty between
us was broken, and it is well known that he
was the instigator of almost all the cruelties
and exactions under which we formerly
laboured, and which he again sought to re-
commence."

"What is his name?" asked the Baron;
" for I wish to be thoroughly acquainted with
every one concerned for or against our
cause."

" The Marchese Phillipo Carignano—a man
implacable in his resentments and hatreds;
but, Baron, the principal business that at present occupies my mind is with respect to your
present visit to Genoa. As you are a perfect stranger you may forward our views
materially by seeking an interview with

Count Domenico Rivalora, who possesses,
although a Corsican by birth, extensive lands
on the Ligurian coast, not far from Genoa.
Though at present undecided, the Count is a
true patriot. His family is a branch of the
house of Rossi, at Parma, illustrious in Italian
history, and his immediate ancestor, Francesco
Rivalora, was raised by the Emperor Maxi-
milian to the dignity of Count Palatine, from
which time the title has remained in the
family. Three of his descendents settled in
Corsica—one in Bastia, one in Calvi, and one
in Ajaccio.

" Count Domenico was always considered
friendly to the Genoese Republic, and was
actually invested with the office of commissary
in Bologna; we, however, have received secret
intelligence that he is disgusted with the conduct of Genoa at breaking the last treaty, and
requires very little further insight into their
conduct to induce him to enter into our
cause. These letters and papers from Paoli,"
and the Signor took a packet from his pocket,

which he gave to the Baron, "you will deliver only to himself, and explain to him
your offers and our terms with you. If he
joins us—and I firmly believe he will—our
success is almost certain, for his influence and
connections in the island, that are now
neutral, will more than counterbalance the
defection of the family of De Matrà."

"I see now," said the Baron ; "much
good may be done by my voyage to Genoa,
where, in point of fact, I must go, for I have
appointed to meet my nephew there on the
first of next month. He is, without excep-
tion, the finest young man in Italy, or anywhere else, for that matter; he will make a
noble soldier. I placed him under the eye of
General D——, one of the ablest tacticians in
the art of war now living. The youth has
served with distinguished success for two
years in the army of Charles Emmanuel. The
moment I reach Genoa and explain to him
my views and intentions, he will embark for
Corsica. I shall entrust him with the money

you at present require; he will bring you letters from me, and I give him to your care, for he is as dear to me as my life."

"He is the very man we want," said the Corsican Chief, rubbing his broad and muscular palms together, while his dark eyes flashed. "Yes, a noble, high-spirited youth, a stranger, well skilled in arms, and enthusiastic in the cause of liberty. In truth, Baron, all is most fortunate. He shall have a distinguished command the moment he arrives. By the bye," and he paused a moment, "yes, it will be better; let him embark from this port, and lay out part of the sum you send in arms and ammunition—yes, ammunition of all things."

"He shall do so," said the Baron. "I intended that he should embark from either this port or Nice; it will answer better from here, as arms and ammunition can be obtained in any quantities. When I have seen Count Domenico Rivalora I shall embark immediately for Tunis, as I before stated to you;

thence I shall return with my first supply of arms, &c., and by the latter end of July, or August at farthest, you may expect me in Corsica with the stipulated force, &c."

"You perfectly understand the situation, &c., of the various ports I have pointed out to you?" said the Corsican, folding up the map they had been carefully examining. "You had better take it," he continued, giving the map to the Baron. "You will find them all marked, as well as the way laid down from each port, into the interior of the island. All the places, towns, and forts, &c., in our hands are also noted. I must now proceed to Pisa, for I have much to talk over, as well as much to settle with the Signor Gratiano."

The Corsican arose, and threw his large mantle over his broad shoulders. The Baron took the map, and held out his hand to the Chief, saying—

"Our interview has, I trust, been as satisfactory to you as to myself."

The Corsican grasped De Newhoff's hand cordially.

"Yes," he returned, "quite as gratifying, and I wish with all my heart that you may meet with all the success you deserve, that you will find your nephew well, and that he may prove a comfort to you, and a great help to our cause."

And the two parted, mutually pleased with each other.

CHAPTER VI.

BARON DE NEWHOFF started at once for Genoa, but as there were no steamers at that time, there was no commanding the winds and the waves. After struggling for two days against a high and contrary wind, the felucca in which he had embarked was forced to put into the Gulf of Spezzia. The Baron was greatly vexed at the delay, and considering the large sum he had paid for his passage, got tired of the vessel. Having landed, and finding it too late to proceed that evening, he sent for a muleteer and bargained for a couple of mules to take him the following day through Chiavare. He took up his quarters for the night at a first-rate hotel, and having ordered his supper, sat down to it with an appetite, and consoled himself by soliloquising:

" After all I shall not lose much time, for as we pass through Chiavare I can call upon the Count Rivalora and execute my commission with him."

So, having satisfied his appetite and eased his mind, he retired to rest, ordering his muleteer to be ready for service.

The road, if indeed it could be called a road, was an extraordinary zigzag path, which, like a huge sea serpent, wound sometimes through the deep sea sands, then into a roaring torrent, impetuous, but not deep; then, by way of variety, right across the summit of the highest hills; and very high hills they are that stretch from Spezzia beyond Genoa.

If the Baron found the road detestable, the beauty of the scenery from Spezzia almost to Sestri di Sevante was frequently magnificent, though wild and scarcely cultivated, for the land, though luxuriant in natural and sweet scented plants and trees, is absolutely sterile. It was with the utmost difficulty the traveller contrived to perform the ten leagues between Spezzia and Lestri in one day, though his guide forced him to rise with the sun.

The whole line of coast he traversed presented a singular feature, which struck the Baron forcibly. Nature was as ostentatious as it was luxuriant; every plant was a flower; every tree a laurel; but not one single bud or production that serves to sustain life was to be seen; whilst everything to embellish grew in profusion.

The next day De Newhoff left early, intending to visit Chiavare that evening, but a tremendous storm in the hills, which lasted six hours, so flooded the mountain torrents that he was forced to halt at a miserable *venta*, near the foot of a stupendous hill, at whose base ran a stream more like a mighty river than an insignificant rivulet, which it had been before the commencement of the storm ; but so it is with all the streams running from

the Maritime Alps into the Mediterranean.
Their beds, covered with huge rocks and
stones, are many of them a quarter of a mile
across, with a shallow stream winding through
the middle, not twenty yards wide.   After a
storm the entire bed of these mountain streams
are covered with a raging flood, and many
lives are annually sacrificed by the sudden
manner in which the torrent descends.

Whilst the baron was gazing discontentedly
at the discoloured and raging flood that boldly
breasted the calm waters of the Mediterranean, for, though the thunders rolled in
hollow murmurs amid the hills, and a black
pall hung, as it were, over their summits,
on the broad bosom of the sea the sun shone
brightly, and the light southerly wind played
along its surface—a great contrast to the time
when the Baron was attempting to make his
way to Genoa.

As De Newhoff was gazing on the flood,
and calculating how long it might last, he
perceived, advancing towards the venta, at

the door of which he was standing, three persons and two mules coming down the road he
had returned from in the morning. One was
placed on the back of one of the mules; the
two others were supporting him, one on each
side. The landlord, happening to come out
at the moment and catching sight of those
approaching, exclaimed,

"*Eh! per Christo!* they are the travellers
bound for Genoa, who started from here,
signor, before you arrived. I thought by
their not returning they must have crossed the
river before the storm; but, *Santa Madonna!*
something must have happened;" and away he
ran to meet the strangers.

As the travellers approached, the Baron eyed
them with some degree of curiosity. They
were all three dripping wet. The signor who
sat upon the mule appeared hurt, looking exceedingly pale and very weak. The Baron
approached and courteously offered to assist,
expressing a hope that the signor had not met
with any very serious accident.

" Only somewhat bruised, half drowned, and more than a little frightened," replied the stranger, " and all owing to my own rashness and want of patience."

He was assisted to alight by one of the persons who supported him, and who appeared like an attendant; the other was the muleteer. Bowing to the Baron, the two entered the *venta*.

The stranger who was injured was a tall, thin man, about fifty years of age, and of a very remarkable physiognomy. His attendant was younger, shorter, and stouter, with an extremely sharp, intelligent countenance, but withal shrewd, and somewhat marked by a cunning cast of the eye.

" How did the accident happen ?" asked the Baron of the muleteer, who was busily engaged unstrapping the luggage of the strangers.

" No fault of mine, signor," replied the man, continuing his occupation; " the signor, who I think is a priest, or something belonging to Mother Church, was more obstinate than a mule, and persisted in crossing the stream, and we ascended the mountain to look for a less dangerous ford, although I knew it was useless, and I told him so. He said he was in a hurry, having already lost valuable time, and would try to cross the torrent. Blessed Saints! it was a miracle he was not drowned. I warned him of the danger, but he heeded me not; and he was washed off the mule in an instant, and only that he was dashed against a rock, and held on till we pulled him out, we should never have seen more of him—he would have been swept into the sea; but here comes the rain."

The Baron seeing there was nothing for it but patience, retired to the small chamber in which his baggage had been deposited, and throwing himself into a chair, took a pocket map from his vest, and began examining it, when he distinctly heard voices in the adjoining chamber in conversation. He would have paid no attention to the circumstance, but he was astonished to hear that they conversed in German ; the partition between the rooms was a very thin wood panel. The first sentence he caught was—

" I fear, padre, you are more seriously injured than you imagined, and will not be able to proceed for some days."

" My son," replied a much weaker voice, " the pains of the body must not be thought of when the welfare of our Holy Church is at stake.'

The Baron was on the point of giving some intimation of his near presence, but an unaccountable feeling of curiosity took possession of him, and he allowed them to continue their conversation.

" True, padre, true ; as you always tell me, everything must be sacrificed that stands in the way of Holy Church's welfare or aggrandisement. Still, if you fall ill and get worse, our project falls to the ground. By patiently waiting a few days, you will regain strength ; you have already overtaxed your powers of endurance."

" Not so, my son; but even if I fall, we must persevere. We have been led astray; had we not been misinformed of the movements of the young Count de Briesbach—"

At the mention of his nephew's name, the Baron sat like one electrified; the speaker continued:

" We should have avoided all this. It was said he had gone to Modena, and when too late, we received intelligence that it was to Genoa. This has caused us untoward delay, added to the great and inconvenient round we were forced to take to enable us to reach that city. The Count may have left Genoa, and how far and where he may have gone, it is impossible to say; but he must not be permitted to escape us; this rich inheritance must not be lost to the church; it would be evil enough to lose it under any circumstances, but to see it go into the hands of a heretic—the saints forbid! Even now, Heinrick, I feel better for this rubbing. How

fortunate that we brought this salve with us.
Please the Virgin, I hope we shall be able
to resume our journey to-morrow. One day
more, or a day and a half at farthest, will
finish our journey ; for I am told the road is
much better for chaises to Genoa. Go, my
son, and procure some food, for I feel both
weak and faint."

The Baron remained in a state of complete
bewilderment for some minutes after the
voices ceased. What had his nephew to do
with the church and a rich inheritance ? Who
were the priests ? whence did they come, and
what was their purpose with Otho de Briesbach ? The only thing he could clearly
make out of the whole was that whoever the
strangers were, their intention evidently was
to secure for the Church of Rome an inheritance intended for a heretic, and yet all this
was a mystery to the Baron.

"Is Otho about to be married to some
wealthy heiress," he thought, " and are these

pious padres anxious to prevent the marriage? for in no other way can the youth become possessed of a rich inheritance."

The Baron relapsed into silence, and sat for a considerable time in deep thought ; all at once a new and more tangible idea struck him.

" Can it be possible that the Baron de Hammerstein and his two sons are dead ? They were all rigid Catholics. In default of male heir, the vast property passed to the Church. Otho is the heir, for I believe neither of the young men had children. This must be seen to. Who are these priests ?— Jesuits, I expect—and what is their object? Do they follow Otho for the purpose of removing him—perhaps murdering him—to obtain this vast property."

Again the Baron became silent, for he had given utterance to his thoughts in a low whisper. He was greatly puzzled ; but the result of his meditation was a determination, before he went to bed, to write to a friend at

Frankfort, and ascertain from him if anything fatal had occurred in the Hammerstein family. He also determined not to lose sight of the priest until he had seen Otho, to put him on his guard.

The Baron contrived very cleverly to start the following morning at the same time as the strangers, for whether the salve which the priest used to rub on his bruises was exceedingly good, or that mental anxiety was more powerful than bodily suffering, the stranger mounted his mule to all appearance completely restored, excepting that his naturally pale complexion looked somewhat more yellow, and his bright and searching eye less brilliant.

De Newhoff thought the stranger appeared vexed when he enquired courteously after· his wounds, saying in an indifferent and easy tone,

"I rejoice at having been so fortunate as to have a companion on this solitary route; we travel the same road, I believe."

The stranger bowed courteously enough, saying,

" I fear you will find me a dull companion and a very slow traveller."

" In truth," replied the Baron, smiling, " if ever so much inclined for quick locomotion, neither the road nor the animals would admit of any other pace than a walk."

As the travellers entered the now shallow stream of the torrent of the previous day, the Baron remarked,

" Had I not witnessed the broad and furi-ous flood, I should have disbelieved any one who had told me that so insignificant a rivulet could, in the course of an hour, have defied the passage of the boldest horseman."

" I was nearly paying very dearly for my disbelief, signor," said the stranger; " I have not been accustomed to witness such results from a mere thunder storm."

" The streams from these Alps are very different indeed from the almost gentle rivers flowing into the lordly Rhine," remarked the Baron, carelessly.

The Priest turned on his saddle, so as to be able to fix his keen eyes upon the Baron's face, as he said,

" You have visited, or probably resided in Germany, signor?" and then added : " Though you speak Italian fluently, I should say you were not a native ; more likely German or Russian."

" Neither one nor the other, signor," replied the Baron, smiling. " I passed a good deal of my time in Germany some years ago, and am tolerably well acquainted with the country bordering the Rhine, from Cologne to Coblentz. Have you, signor, ever visited that beautiful line of country, with its majestic stream, its glorious banks, and its hundred picturesque castles ? some, like old Drachenfels, towering to the skies."

" I have been in Germany, and have both ascended and descended the noble river you

speak of," quietly replied the stranger;
" there is in truth but little resemblance between this track of country and the hills of
the Rhine. Still, we have nothing to com-
plain of, for there is much beauty in this
coast scenery; besides, on our left we have
the sparkling and broad sea in compensation
for the rapid waters of the Rhine. Did you
know any of the possessors of those noble
mansions to be seen studding the country
from Bonn to Linz?"

" I am acquainted," said the Baron, " with
one or two noblemen residing within a few
leagues of Drachenfels."

" Indeed," said the stranger; " then it is
probable we may know the same persons. In
travelling, how strange sometimes are these
chance encounters. Without being inquisi-
tive, signor, might I enquire the name of my
travelling companion? Mine is Orsini; I am
a native of the Eternal City."

" A noble and ancient name, signor, and a
proud birth-place. I drew my breath in an

island, famous more for its wealth and commerce than its historical recollections, though
we have them also—I mean England—and
my name is Philip Maunsel. We are a
rambling race when once we leave our iron
bound shores.   I think I may say an Englishman is to be met with in every part of the
inhabited globe."

"An Englishman," repeated the Signor
Orsini; and again a keen, enquiring glance
shot from beneath the long, dark, drooping
eyelashes of the Italian.   "I was saying we
may probably know the same persons, for I
also have spent much time in Germany, and
resided many months with the Count Von
Koningsbergern, near Coblentz. Did you ever
meet that nobleman?"

"No," said the Baron, " I never heard the
name; I resided for months at a time in
Frankfort, where I was intimately acquainted
with the Count de Mannheim, and was staying with him at the time he was completing
the purchase he had made of a picturesque

spot on the borders of the Rhine, a hunting tower belonging to a young nobleman of the name of Otho de Breisbach, whose uncle, the Baron de Hammerstein, possessed vast estates, I believe, near to the Tower, which De Mannheim told me was in a very dilapidated condition."

" I know both the place and the persons you mention quite well," said the stranger, without perceptible sign of either surprise or emotion on his placid pale features. " The Baron de Hammerstein I have frequently met; he is a member of the Catholic Church, and had two—very fine young men—sons. It is scarcely two months since I saw the Baron at Linz; so you see, Signor Maunsel, we are scarcely strangers to each other, knowing the same persons in far off lands."

" Humph!" muttered the Baron to himself, " it's very strange ; this rich inheritance is scarcely that of the Hammersteins, or else this man is an admirable actor. Time—time, however, will tell."

Changing the conversation, he pointed out to the Italian the town of Chiavare, standing on one side of a river, and the village of Lavagna—the name also of the river—occupying the other.

"That town is well situated, and appears very large. How different is the aspect of this fertile plain to the country we have hitherto traversed," observed the Italian.

"There is a splended species of stone found here," said their guide, " called Pretra de Lavagna ; it is harder than marble, and of a most beautiful black. You may reach Parma from this town," continued the guide, " by a very good open road, passing by Varese, the whole distance not exceeding twelve leagues."

"I wish I had known that," said Signor Orsini, turning to his attendant, who rode close beside him, "We came from Modena, and have made a considerable circuit, which might have been avoided had I heard of the road."

" Ah! signor," replied the guide, "it is not the interest of the muleteers or the *albergistes* to put travellers on that road. At all events, you have seen a great deal more of the country."

" And paid a great deal more for the seeing it, *amico*," said the Italian, in a quiet tone; " but here we are."

They passed over the the long and very steep bridge crossing the Lavagna, and entered the then busy and commercial town of Chiavare. At the Eiu d'Or, the best hotel, the travellers stopped, and the Baron enquired of the Italian how long he proposed halting at Chiavare; as the day was yet young they could easily reach Sestri di Levante that night; that he had to visit a nobleman who resided close to the town ; but that two hours would be sufficient for him, and that he should feel much pleasure in continuing the journey in his company.

" I should be equally pleased, Signor, " said the Italian; " but I am sorely pressed for time. I shall not stop more than ten minutes, to procure fresh mules and a guide; I wish to reach Genoa to-night. It is only eight leagues from hence."

"After your accident," remarked the Baron, " will not the ride be too much for you?"

"Not at all," replied the Signor Orsini; " they were travelling bruises. Besides, I have pressing business."

" Ha!" muttered the Baron to himself, "he wants to get rid of me ; but he shall not do so easily."

" Well," said De Newhoff, aloud," I will not lose so agreeable a companion if I can help it."

Orsini made an inclination of the head, but no other reply.

" I can procure horses here," continued the Baron, "and will do my best to overtake you, so adieu for the present."

While the Italian was arranging for fresh mules, and paying his guide, the Baron enquired of the landlord where the mansion of the Count de Rivalora was situated.

" Not five minutes' walk from the west end of the town, Signor. You cannot make any mistake, for it is the first residence on the right hand, on the road to Genoa, after quitting the town."

Placing his packet of letters in his vest, the Baron set off, without taking any other refreshment than a glass of wine and a biscuit.

CHAPTER VII.

No sooner was the Baron out of sight than Signor Orsini and his attendant entered a private chamber of the hotel.   Carefully shutting the door, the attendant said to his master, who had seated himself in a chair,

" Now, holy father, what is to be done? What a fatality to stumble upon this meddling Baron de Newhoff.   He is on his way to join his nephew, I have no doubt.   He, however, knows nothing of us, nor has he the most remote idea of our being anything else than mere travellers."

" I don't know that—I don't know that," said the priest, rather sharply : " had we not picked up the letter addressed to him, and which, it seems, he has not missed, he would assuredly have deceived us. His commencing a conversation at once leading to persons and things in Germany looks suspicious. I recollect, too, we had apartments adjoining those he occupied at that miserable *venta* where we were forced to sleep last night. The partition was very slight between the rooms. He might have heard our conversation. We had then no suspicion, and as we spoke in German, we thought ourselves safe."

"But, holy father, we must adopt some plan by which he will be prevented joining us again. It will never do to let him enter Genoa with us. We must baffle him there. However, he may not have the slightest suspicion of who we are."

"But," said the Jesuit, after a moment's thought, "if he does not overtake us on the road, his suspicions will be aroused."

A knock at the door caused the priest to pause. The landlord entered.

" Strange to say, signor, there are no fresh mules to be had. I have sent all over the town, in vain; a large party of Lombard packmen from Parma swept the town of every available animal. There is, however, a most favourable opportunity, signor, if you do not dislike the sea. A fine felucca will put to sea in a few minutes. I have sent to stay the *padrone*, till I had spoken to you. The wind is highly favourable, and you will reach Genoa in less than four hours.''

" How fortunate !" exclaimed both master and attendant, starting eagerly up, and thanking the landlord.

" It is the very thing," said the priest, " for I am much fatigued with my journey, and I can rest on board the felucca."

In a few minutes the Jesuit and his attendant, with two men to carry their luggage, took the road to the beach, and in ten minutes more the felucca, with a fine breeze from the eastward, was rapidly making the best of her way for Genoa.

In less than four hours, the felucca was safely at anchor in the noble and spacious harbour of Genoa. Putting their baggage into a small boat, the two voyagers were put on shore, as the dusk of evening fell on the narrow streets and magnificent palaces and mansions of that city of kings. At the principal landing place of the Porta del Mare, several porters stood waiting to be employed. But the Signor Orsini politely declined the services, and, leaving his attendant in charge of their luggage, he wrapped his mantle closely about him, and passing through the immense iron gates, entered the city.

Genoa is now as well-known to the English as the City of London—perhaps, much better to many. It has a strange and singular appearance to a traveller, on his first visit ; but he soon gets accustomed to its miserably narrow streets, which in rainy weather are inundated by the sheets of water falling from the projecting eaves of mansions of immense

height and appropriate appearance, all
apparently fit for the residence of princes.
There are, however, three or four magnificent
streets, probably not to be surpassed in
Europe for the grandeur of their palaces and
the chaste beauty of their entrances.

The Italian, passing along the lofty wall
bordering the harbour, entered the narrow
street leading into the square of the Annun-
ciata, into which runs the noble street
called Balbi. Striking away to the right, he
plunged into those numerous narrow and
obscure pathways leading from the Piazza
Amorosa. Though enshrouded in the shades
of evening, the pedestrian pursued his way as
correctly as if it had been broad daylight,
and presently stopped in a very deserted
quarter of the city. The street was not more
than fifteen feet broad, and the houses on,
each side were seven or eight stories high;
there were no lamps of any kind; and
except here or there tapers, placed in small
cases, containing the image of some favourite

saint, there was not a glimmer of light to enliven the dark and deserted locality.

The Jesuit at length stopped before a very lofty and gloomy-looking mansion; a shrine to the Virgin, some twenty or thirty paces off, threw a very faint light against the front of this building. Every window appeared closed, and, on the outside, ranges of thick iron bars gave it the look of either a prison or a madhouse. In the massive doorway was fixed an iron ring, which the priest pulled with some difficulty, for it appeared as if it had become fast with rust and want of use.

After the lapse of about five minutes, a slide in the door was pushed back, and through a small iron grating appeared the bald head of a very old man; in his hand he held a lamp. In a rather strong and harsh voice, he demanded, with very little civility, and certainly with no courteousness,

"Who rings?—what do you want, eh?"

The Jesuit, without replying, pushed a small card through the grating, on which were some figures, but no writing. The old man took the card, cast the light of his lamp on it, and immediately bowed very low, saying,

" *Subito, subito, Padre,*" and then a key was turned in the lock, several huge bolts shot back, the ponderous door swung open, and the priest entered. The old man again bowed very low, and was shutting the door, when the Jesuit asked,

" Is your son in the house, Ambrosio?"

" He is, Father."

" That is fortunate. Send him at once to the Quay, at the Porte del Mare; he will see a man sitting on two leather trunks. Tell him to enquire of that person if that is the baggage of Signor Orsini. Let him take charge of the trunks, and conduct my attendant here. He is a stranger to this city."

The old man closed the hall door without locking it, and said,

" Let me first show you to your apartments, Father; for it is a good step to the kitchen. I will also tell my wife to make ready your supper. Your room is all prepared, for we have been expecting you for the last week."

Passing along the lofty and unfurnished hall, they came to a spiral stone staircase, ascending to the first story. The old man threw open a door, and they entered a large and well-furnished saloon, though, it is true, the articles were of some antiquity. Several large pictures in cumbrous frames hung on the walls, all of which were covered with green baize. At the further end, facing the fire-place, was a kind of altar, on which stood a silver crucifix, with the body of the Saviour cast in the same metal, the whole above three feet in height. Several books, richly bound, lay upon a table.

Lighting a handsome antique lamp, the old man, after bowing very low, retired, saying,

" Your reverence shall have supper almost immediately. Your attendant shall not be long absent;" and pointing to a door, continued, " that, Holy Father, leads to your and your attendant's sleeping chamber."

Left alone, the Jesuit threw aside his mantle, placed a packet of letters upon the table, and then, with his hands behind his back, paced the chamber in a thoughtful and abstracted mood. He was roused by the return of the old domestic, who came back and gave him several letters, saying:

" These, reverend father, I received at the place indicated to me, and I have done every-thing in my power to obey the instructions you sent me by letter."

" Good," said the priest, looking over the backs of the letters. " How long has the Count de Briesbach been in Genoa ?"

" Up to this afternoon, he had not arrived, Padre," replied the old man.

" Not arrived !" replied the priest. " That is scarcely possible. The Count left Turin ten days since and took the direct road to Genoa."

" Then, father, he must travel by another

name; for no such person as the Count de
Briesbach has put up at any of the hotels in
this city; of that I am certain. My son and
I have never failed a single day to make
cautious enquiries. We strictly examined the
albergos of San Pietro d'Arena, and even
the *locandas* of the second class, but no one
is acquainted with the name of the Count de
Briesbach."

" Very strange, and to me unaccountable,"
said the priest. " Is there any news of im-
portance talked about in Genoa?"

" Yes, your reverence, there has been considerable interest, as well as indignation,
excited all through the city, especially
amongst the higher classes, by the stoppage
of the Countess di Sera's carriage by a noted
brigand on the Bochetta. The Countess was
plundered of all her baggage and jewels; but
worst of all, the brigands carried off her
daughter or her ward, and intend keeping
her captive in the mountains till an immense
ransom has been paid."

" The brigands of the Bochetta are becoming dangerous, and should be put down," said the priest.

" They say also that a young signor was riding in company with the Countess, who, with two of the brigands and one of the *gens d'armes*, was killed. But this part of the intelligence requires confirmation, for the signor's body has not been found, though the postillions declare they saw him shot and fall over the cliff."

" How long is it since this occurred?" asked the Jesuit, eagerly fixing his penetrating eyes on the dim grey orbs of the old domestic.

" Let me see," and he began counting the days of the week on his fingers. " Yes,— yesterday—eight days exactly."

" Then most likely it must be so," said the priest, and even in his sallow, pale cheek a slight sign of colour was perceptible. " That signor was the Count de Briesbach. It is not likely, however, that he was killed, more probably detained a prisoner. Leave me now, Ambrosio, and send up my attendant the moment he arrives."

The old man bowed, saying :

" How soon will your reverence like to have supper ?"

" As soon as possible; but let it be a frugal repast,—something very simple and plainly cooked."

The old man retired.

CHAPTER VIII.

OTHO DE BRIESBACH calculated that with his
own good steed he could very well accompany
his new acquaintance as far as Campomarino,
a distance of some thirty miles. He therefore rose at an early hour and saw that the
animal was well fed and groomed, and then
joined the ladies at breakfast.

"We shall, at all events," said the Countess, "have a remarkably fine day. As you
are a stranger, Count, to this part of the
country, you will enjoy some of the scenery.
From the summit of the Bochetta you will
have a splendid view, if the atmosphere con-
tinues as clear as it is now. It struck me

last night, just after you left us, that your horse will not carry you further than Voltazzio without rest."

" I am told," said the Count, " it is only about thirty miles from here to Campomarino, at the foot of the mountain on the other side. Your stopping for an hour at Voltazzio for refreshment will be quite sufficient for my horse. He has done harder service, with the chance of being shot into the bargain."

" Did that handsome animal you rode yesterday carry you into battle ?" asked Vannina, " if so you must be very much attached to it."

" And so I am, fair lady," said the Count ; " that is the identical horse which carried me across the river to attack those marauders infesting your convent during the late war."

" If you will accept a seat in our carriage from Campomarino," said the Countess, " one of my attendants can bring on your horse the following day ; thus you will save passing a lonely evening at so dull a place. It is distant from Genoa four posts."

To this arrangement the Count most willingly acceded, and immediately after breakfast the party left Novi. They were to be joined by four *gens d'armes* at Voltazzio, from which town the ascent of the Bochetta commences. Excepting the strong fortress of Gavi, perched upon a rocky eminence, there was nothing very remarkable to attract the attention of the travellers. From the nature of the road they travelled slowly, and the Count enjoyed riding by the side of the open carriage, in conversation with the ladies most part of the way to Voltazzio.

After an hour's rest and refreshment, accompanied by four tall and powerful *gens d'armes*, well mounted and armed, the party left Voltazzio and commenced the ascent of the highest mountain in the range of the Maritime Alps. As you mount, a wilder or more desolate scene it is impossible to see.

"A charming place for brigands," said the Countess to our hero, as he rode by the side of the carriage with his gaze fixed, we are bound to admit, oftener upon the sparkling eyes and animated features of Vannina di Matrà, than on the wild and vast crags that everywhere surrounded them.

"A most unpromising tract to pursue them in," returned Otho; "in fact, regular troops would find it impossible to act amidst such crags and precipices, where every rock afford shelter and security to the robbers to cut off their pursuers."

"That no doubt is the reason they have existed for so many years amid these wilds— almost unmolested, or any attempt made to drive them out," said the Countess, "for no sooner has a wretch committed a crime in Genoa than he goes, as it is styled, 'to take the air of the mountain.' In fact, according to report, the whole range of these wild Alpine passes is populated with runaway galley slaves, assassins, forgers, robbers, and heaven knows, men guilty of every crime capable of being committed."

" These wild crags and precipices," observed Vannina, looking down a tremendous gorge into a wild and sterile valley, many hundred feet below them, "puts me strangely in mind of my own mountain home. I was a mere child when I left it, but I have a perfect re-collection of the wild and magnificent scenery that surrounded our mansion."

At that moment the party was startled by the report of three or four gun shots fired in succession just ahead of them. The *gens-d'armes* and the Countess's attendants unslung their carbines, and the Count hastily drew a pistol from one of the holsters and examined the priming. Just before them was an abrupt angle in the road, turning round the base of a mass of lofty crags. Several more shots came from the other side of the rock. The postillions halted, while the *gens d'armes* galloped rapidly forward and turned the angle of the rock. The Count de Briesbach called loudly and rode forward to restrain them from qui tting their charge, rightly guessing the firing was some subterfuge of the brigands.

" Good heavens, Vannina !" cried the Countess, " this is getting serious. These brigands may be very picturesque at a distance; but really—"

Scarcely had the words been spoken, when, as if by magic, springing from behind innumerable rocks that had concealed them, some twenty lawless ruffians surrounded the carriage, one of whom seized the bridle of Otho's horse ; but paid dearly for it, the Count felling him to the ground with a blow from the butt of his pistol, and spurring his spirited steed, he called to the astonished and frightened domestics to make a dash at the brigands. There was no sign of the return of the *gens d'armes* ; they had evidently fallen into a trap and were secured, for the Count heard two or three rapid shots.

The Countess's attendants were speedily

disarmed, and though the Count shot down
another of the ruffians, to his astonishment
no pistol or carbine was levelled at him, though
several of the men strove eagerly to pull him
from his horse. A wild shriek from the carriage, which was some yards behind, caused
him to spur his horse fiercely ; and striking
down the man who held him, with his dragoon
sabre, which he carried, he pressed through
the crowd of enraged men, who struck at him
with the butts of their carbines; he reached
the carriage just in time to perceive one of
the robbers with Vannina in his arms, hurry-
ing down the steep precipitous rocks that
bordered the road.

Instantly dismounting, in despite of the
efforts of the brigands, though one—enraged at
a wound he had received—fired full in the
face of de Briesbach ; fortunately the piece
flashed in the pan, and the villain bounded
over the side of the road, hotly pursued by
Otho, till, seeing a powerful bandit carrying
Vannina in his arms, with apparently as much

ease as he would have carried a child, instantly gave over the pursuit, and turned his attention to the other robber, who was about a hundred yards in advance.

The path the Count pursued, if path it could be called, was a terrible one—a mere ledge running along the side of a precipice more than six hundred feet deep. Right before the path of the robber was a cascade, foaming and boiling and tumbling over huge masses of rock and sending up into the air a cloud of foam. Otho de Briesbach was a strong, active man, with a determined and unshrinking resolution; but the robber kept the same distance in advance, although carrying Vannina in his arms; but this was owing to being well acquainted with the niceties of the path, evidently one used by the brigands. Otho raised his pistol several times, but hesitated to fire; not that he doubted hitting the maiden and not the robber—for he had no mistrust of his aim; but he feared that in killing or wounding the man both would be hurled into the valley below.

" Well," said the Count, almost breathless, " that cascade will stop the villain ;" but just as he reached the edge the brigand stopped. Ourhero could perceive Vannina struggling in his arms, and he advanced eagerly to within three or four paces of the robber, who, holding Vannina firmly with one hand, presented a horse-pistol with the other, with a savage curse, at the breast of the Count. At the instant a loud and startling voice exclaimed—

" Hold! on your life hold your fire, Pietro," and with an active bound, a man sprung from an adjoining rock, and leaped upon the narrow ledge on which the robber stood.

Otho held his pistol still extended; the stranger turned round and looked him full in the face, saying—

" *Mille Diavolo*, Count, we have met sooner than I anticipated."

Otho seemed confounded, for before him

stood his travelling companion of the day previous.

"And just in the nick of time," continued the stranger. "Put up your pistol, Pietro, and let the lady have the protection of that signor's arm to the caverns. Did I not tell you on no account to fire upon this gentleman?"

"Body of me, captain!" exclaimed the man named Pietro; "what would you have me do? By my soul, it was getting a nice point between us; if I did not shoot him he'd have shot me to a certainty;" and letting go the maiden, he put his pistol back into his belt.

Vannina no sooner found herself free than she sprung to the side of De Briesbach, with an exclamation of intense joy.

"Dear lady," said the Count, placing the arm of the fair girl within his, "I know you are greatly and justly terrified; but as long as life is left me no hurt shall come to you."

"Oh! signor, I have no fear now; till I

saw you following us my heart nearly failed
me, and I do believe that had I not been so
firmly held, I should have thrown myself
over the precipice sooner than remain alone
in the hands of these brigands."

The captain of the band, who had stood
apart conversing in a low tone with the
man Pietro, now approached the Count,
who saw, as he looked round, several of the
men who had plundered the Countess's carriage, descending the rocks by different
paths.

" Count," said the Captain, " I can say but
few words to you now; but of this rest as-
sured, neither you nor that lady shall receive
the slightest hurt or insult. We must proceed to our retreat; she shall remain under
your care."

" Thank God!" murmured Vannina; and
the Count could feel the little arm that rested
on his tremble.

" Where I shall take you and the lady,"
continued the Captain; "there will be none of

my comrades in the same cave, only a middle-aged woman and a very young girl. Are you content with my word, Count? I owe you gratitude for a life preserved. I may say I have saved yours, but still I consider myself your debtor."

" Is it impossible to restore this lady to her friends to-night ? For myself, I will remain your hostage till any sum you demand is faithfully paid."

" I tell you, Count," said the Captain, firmly, but in a kindly tone, " it is utterly impossible. You see my comrades are gathering around ; I pray you follow me, for "— and he sunk his voice to a very low tone—" I am not the only captain in the expedition. Marco Remini is a blood-thirsty and ferocious man. I would not wish him to see this lady, so follow me, and shelter your fair friend from the water of the cascade as well as you can as we pass through the spray. She will have her luggage in less than half an hour."

Otho de Briesbach hesitated for one mo-

ment, as he looked round and counted more
than fifteen of the robbers approaching in
various directions.

" Do not hesitate, Count, " whispered
Vannina. " I have faith, indeed I have, in
that man's words; he means you well. How
very fortunate was your chance meeting with
him."

" It must be so, dear lady," said Otho, putting his pistol in his vest; "we must bend to
circumstances. You have a noble courage,
thank God, and I trust a few hours, at most a
couple of days, will release you from this
trial."

The captain of the robbers moved forward
alone, Pietro having descended a steep cliff,
and was out of sight. It required some nerve
to follow the robber chief ; the cascade
threw a sheet of spray over the two as they
approached, and actually passed beneath its
splendid arch, which fell over their heads in
the form of a vast bow, and striking a range
of rocks some eighty or a hundred feet below,

shot a cloud of foam of dazzling whiteness into the air.

Otho de Briesbach pressed the fair girl, who shewed no sign of fear, close to his side as they trod the narrow, slippery ledge that ran along the perpendicular cliff, over which shot the cascade, which, falling into the valley below, wound from thence through the plain of Campomarino, and then became lost in the waters of the Mediterranean.

After passing through this thick, wetting, spray of the cascade, the uproar of which was deafening, the Count spoke some words of encouragement to the fair girl, though in truth she braved the terrors of the passage with singular nerve.

" Oh! signor, all this is nothing; the body only suffers here. If alone with these men, to go all through all this, my torture of mind would indeed have been great. But where on earth does this singular robber intend taking us, for I do not see how we can advance twenty yards further. Look! he has stopped."

They approached the Captain, who stood on the edge of a very limited plat-form, looking over its side.

"Your dangerous journey ends here, signora," said the Captain. "Lady, you have great courage and good nerve, as well as your protector, the Count; for I have never yet seen anyone, except our own men, attempt the precipice down which you, Count, so fearlessly plunged. I watched you, fearing lest you might overtake Pietro, one of the boldest and strongest men in our gang, or that he would lose temper and do mischief. I was forced, at the risk of my own neck, to descend by a very dangerous track, to enable me to cut you short before you could reach him."

"I trust no harm was done to the Countess di Sera?" asked Vannina, in a timid, anxious manner.

"No further harm, signora, than the loss of her baggage, and whatever articles of value she possessed. She was allowed to pursue her journey. I did not stay to see her depart, but I know my orders were strictly obeyed."

" What became of the *gens d'armes?*" demanded the Count. " Had it not been for their inconsiderate conduct, this catastrophe could not have occurred. They undoubtedly allowed themselves to be led into a snare."

" It was done," replied the captain, " principally to save shedding blood. You are wrong, however, in supposing this would not have happened, for there were nearly thirty men, not easily to be frightened, on the road. Had you and the *gens d'armes* shewn fight together, the men would most certainly have been shot."

" Perhaps," said the Count, drily. " I have seen greater odds, and not despaired; but what became of them?"

" They were thrown from their horses by ropes stretched across that narrow pass, through which they so heedlessly galloped, and secured with very trifling bruises."

While the robber spoke, a head suddenly

appeared over the side of the cliff. It was one of the brigands, who, addressing the Captain, said,

" If the signora is afraid of the ladder, we can sling a large basket, with ropes."

Otho advanced to the edge of the cliff, and perceived that a long ladder of ropes, secured with iron pins to the fissures in the perpendicular cliff upon which they stood, had been prepared for their descent to a lower platform, some fifty or sixty feet down.

" You had better carry the lady down that ladder, Count," said the Captain.

" There appears to be no other way of descending. Will you trust yourself to me, dear lady ?" said Otho.

The colour was bright upon the maiden's cheek, as she replied,

" I have brought you into trouble, Count, and fear I must continue a burden to you; for I assuredly do not think I could descend that ladder alone."

The Count wrapped Vannina's mantle

tightly around her, and lifting her tenderly and carefully—though we must confess the lady was not one of those unsubstantial beings, light as a feather, but real, substantial flesh and blood — carried her safely down the ladder, and on gaining the platform beheld a tall, middle-aged woman, with a countenance rather prepossessing than otherwise, waiting to receive them.

The Count and Vannina followed the woman into the entrance of an immense cavern, from which they could perceive that numerous others branched off in various directions. Passing into one of these, they were surprised to see it arranged into a very comfortable species of chamber. The sides were hung with matting, a large iron lamp was suspended from the roof, twenty feet above their heads; a fire blazed in a regular chimney place, and the smoke was carried off by an aperture above. A table of oak, and several chairs of the same material were also there.

"This is my chamber, and a small one adjoining contains a bed," said the Captain, entering with them; "this woman will sleep within with the signora, who can occupy this room during the day. You and I, Count, will find quarters in another cave on the opposite side. Where is little Jacqueline?" he he asked, turning to the woman.

"Within, lying on the bed; she is not quite well," replied the female, in a very gentle tone of voice. "Will you follow me, signora?" she continued, addressing Vannina. "Your trunks are already brought, and you can change your clothes, which I fear are very wet."

Vannina looked at the Count for a moment as if hesitating, and the brigand seeming to guess her thoughts, said, speaking in a kind but serious tone—

"You may let your mind rest in peace; excepting that you will for a few days be separated from your relatives and friends. In every other respect you will be as safe here as if you were at home. Now, Count, follow me; in an hour you can rejoin the lady here and partake of some refreshment. As for myself, I shall not intrude upon the privacy of the lady till I have the pleasure of restoring her to her family."

Respectfully saluting the fair hand held out to him, the Count retired with the Captain into the outward cavern, which also contained a wide fire-place and every kind of article arranged in great order and cleanliness for the purposes of cooking. A massive oak table and half-a-dozen wooden benches completed its furniture.

"This range of caverns," said the brigand to the Count, "is appropriated to the use of myself, my lieutenant, and ten men; but during your stay, only Pietro, the man you have already seen, will remain here. Three hundred yards below us is a much greater extent of caverns, extending within the mountains, perhaps more than a mile; and when you examine the situation of these extraordinary caverns, more than seven hundred feet above the level of the valley below, and not to be attained by strangers, except with immense labor and great danger, you will see how difficult any attempt would be to dislodge us.   Besides, these caverns have other outlets; and so well known to us are the valleys and gorges of these mountains, that we could as easily baffle an army as the Protestant chief of the Camissards in Languedoc resisted the troops sent against him, a few years ago, by the French King, who found it impossible to drive that chief out of his mountain fastnesses."

"But they might surround you, and cut you off from all supplies," said the Count; "and it strikes me as most astonishing, that a powerful state like Genoa should submit to such an astounding state of things; that a robber force should actually dwell amid the very hills that back their city, infest their only road, I may say, into the interior of the country, and by which road all their inland commerce is carried on. Altogether the knowledge amazes me."

"You will be more amazed then, signor Count," returned the brigand, a little sharply, "when I tell you that actually within the very walls of Genoa, there exists, at this present hour, a gang of regular assassins— not robbers—but systematic assassins—an organised establishment, with their chief, and that a scale of charges, according to rank, station, or risk, is laid down."

"Indeed, I am more than amazed," said the Count.

"Thus, you see, Count, a man can gratify his malice or vengance on any one who has offended him, or get an heir removed, who is in the way of his succession, for a few gold pieces, and without running scarcely any risk himself."

"Then the sooner so corrupt a Republic is blotted out of the states of Europe the better," said the Count.

"That period is not very far distant," replied the Captain; " the Republic now groans under the tyranny of Austria. There will be a popular tumult one of these days, a last spark springing up out of the smouldering ashes of past glory to sink afterwards into utter nothingness."

Otho de Briesbach looked with some surprise at the robber, saying—

"Could not you turn your talents and energies into a—"

" Come, come, Count," hastily interrupted the brigand chief, " say nothing more now; another time, perhaps, before we part, you may wile away an hour listening to some passages in my life. I never was good for much, even from my earliest recollections; now, however, I must leave you. I will place no restrictions on you; do as you like; you are free as far as ransom is concerned, for I take none from you. I know you will not wish to leave the lady you so gallantly followed to rescue till she is released. Perhaps," and the captain looked fixedly in the

Count's face, " you will not refuse a flask of
wine to-night, and take it in my company; I
shall then be able to inform you of our arrangements with respect to the lady's
ransom."

" No," said the Count, " I shall not refuse
your offer. You have, at all events, acted
generously and kindly towards the lady, and
I feel grateful for it; for, in truth, it might
have been much worse."

" If you knew all, Count," said the robber,
as he left the cave, " you would not only say
but think so."

After the departure of the captain of the
brigands, Otho remained wrapped in thought;
the events of the last forty-eight hours made
a strong impression on his mind, and he felt
would, in all probability, have a powerful influence on the rest of his life. We will not
assert that he was, as yet, absolutely in love
with the gentle girl he had done his best to
rescue ; but thus much we may say, she occupied most of his thoughts, and that she

deeply interested him, not only by her exceeding beauty of face and form, but by the
endurance and firmness she displayed, considering how young she was. The strange
situation into which they had been thrown
would, undoubtedly, add to the mutual feeling they already felt for each other, and it
was very evident to the Count that when the
time came for them to separate, he would feel
that he was no long as heart whole as before
he met this Corsican maiden.

From this train of thought he was roused
by the entrance of the woman to whose care
Vannina was entrusted.

"Signor," said the female, "the lady has
changed her dress and wishes to see you,
while I go to prepare some refreshments."

The Count looked into this woman's features,
whom he supposed to be the wife of one of the
brigands. He thought he perceived in her
countenance an appearance of great care; her
age might be about forty-seven, or, perhaps,
fifty; her hair was still black and untouched by

time ; her eyes dark and somewhat wandering
in their expression. Altogether, there was
nothing disagreeable or repulsive in her look,
and her manner was very quiet and gentle.
The Count proceeded to join Vannina, and
the woman went to her cooking operations.

CHAPTER XI.

OTHO DE BRIESBACH was surprised when he entered the cave, where he expected to find Vannina alone, to perceive a very interesting little girl of ten or eleven years of age seated by her side, and to whom she was talking quite cheerfully. Vannina received the Count with a smile of undisguised pleasure.

" You see," she said, as the Count seated himself by the log fire—for the caves were more or less always cold—" you see I have found a very youthful companion, and a very interesting one, too. This little girl—Jacqueline is her name—is the daughter of the female you have seen, and her mother is, I assure you, a very kind person."

"Have you been in these dismal caves, my poor child, all your life?" asked the Count, speaking kindly, and drawing the child towards him.

The little girl was at first shy and timid; she, however, looked on the handsome face of the Count, and gathering courage from the gentle and kind expression of his features, replied—

"I don't recollect any other home."

"Have you never seen any other place?"

"No; all that I have ever seen of the country is from what I have witnessed from the entrance to the caverns. Mamma tells me I was born a long, long way off."

"I fancy," said Vannina, "from what her mother said to me, that she has seen better days, and was born to a more honest position than a brigand's life. I take an interest in this child," continued Vannina, "and would wish to save the poor thing from the future that appears before her."

"A kind wish, and one that I will do my part in helping you to carry out," said the

Count, putting his hand upon the head of the child, who looked up and smiled a pleasant smile.

"Has that strange man, the captain of these robbers, informed you of how we are to be released from these dismal caverns?"

"How *you* are to be liberated, fair lady," said Otho, with a meaning smile; "I am no longer a captive."

"What can you mean?"

"Simply this, that the captain, from what he calls owing me a debt of gratitude for once saving his life, has told me he will take no ransom from me, and has left me at liberty to depart whenever I please."

A shade of sadness crossed the face of the maiden, as she exclaimed,

"What will become of me?"

"No harm shall reach you."

"Then you will not leave me?"

"Not until I have seen you safe out of the hands of these brigands."

"I know I must be ransomed, but how and when; did the captain tell you?" asked

Vannina, a flush of pleasure taking the place of the shade of sadness on her face.

"As yet, signora, he has not; but this night I expect to learn both the how and the when. This captain is an extraordinary man; but apparently neither unkind nor unwilling to render your situation as little irksome as possible. It appears to me, from some observations of his, that, although he is captain or leader of these brigands, there is another chief, a man called Marco Remini."

"Good Heaven! is it possible!" interrupted Vannina, "can that wretch be amongst them. I heard the Countess name this man as being the chief of ferocious assassins and robbers in the mountains between Alessandria and Aqui. She said he was one of the vilest wretches that ever lived; that he had committed nine murders in Genoa, and had escaped from the galleys. What can he have to do with the troop or gang of this captain? I tremble for our lives."

"Nay, dear lady, do not needlessly alarm

yourself," said the Count. "How unfortunate my mentioning this man's name."

"I know a way out of these caves," observed the little girl, looking up into the sweet face of Vannina, who held the child's hand in hers. "I found it out one day when I was playing, and I showed it to my mamma."

"What did your mamma say when you told her?" asked Otho.

"She said it might be of some use at a future day. Are you afraid of dark caves, lady? Oh! I should so like to go out into green fields and gather flowers, and catch the beautiful butterflies; they come some times in summer to the en trance of the great cavern."

"And so you shall, my child, if your mamma will let you come with me."

"I could not leave dear mamma; may she go, too?"

"Yes, she shall go if she likes. Do you think," Vannina said, turning to Otho and speaking in French, "we could profit by this dear child's intelligence?"

" No, I fear not," said our hero, thoughtfully, speaking in the same language. " We
are in the midst of a frightful range of precipices, and though we might gain the exterior
of these caverns, it appears to me almost impossible that you could ever scale those rocks
or descend into the vale before those in pursuit overtook us."

" Alas! too true," said Vannina, somewhat
despondently, " we must wait our time. I
am sincerely grateful to Providence in having you to protect and advise me; for otherwise how terrible would be my thoughts and
feelings in these dismal caverns. Besides,
but for the unaccountable feeling this robber
captain entertains for you, we should have
fared very differently."

" At first I considered his kindness proceeded from my having been instrumental in
saving his life when we were attacked by
those Austrian marauders; but I have since
imagined that, after becoming acquainted with
my name, a change has taken place in his

manner. As I told you once before, I believe he has been differently placed, for when he pleases he has the manner and the appearance of one accustomed to mix in better society than we have found him in," added the Count, with a smile. " Another circumstance also comes to my memory. When I met him on the road, he inquired whether such a carriage as that you travelled in had passed me. Now, that convinces me the stoppage of the Countess di Sera's carriage was a premeditated scheme, and decided on some time previous to the attack. Yet, singular enough, this man, when parting from me at the gates of Novi, said, 'Pray tell the Countess the safest road to Genoa lies through Alessandria and Aqui, which advice, if followed, would have prevented this catastrophe.

" Very true," thoughtfully replied Vannina. " The Countess, before she left Turin, was advised to take that road, and she merely considered the brigand's message a repetition of the same advice."

"Another thing surprises me," said the Count; "why did they not carry off the Countess di Sera? Perhaps they thought you were her daughter, and that the mother would stake her whole wealth to save her child."

"That thought struck me," said Vannina; "perhaps they think so still. Have you any idea of the amount of ransom likely to be demanded for me?" asked Vannina, with a smile. "In truth I shall value myself more highly than I have hitherto done; for I suspect it will cost my dear father a very large sum, and my friends a great deal of trouble."

The Count was uttering some very gallant reply to the fair Corsican, when the female entering informed him that the Captain was in the outer cave, and desired to see him. Wishing the young lady a good night's rest after all her fatigue and perils, he respectfully saluted the fair hand held out to him.

Otho de Briesbach proceeded to meet the brigand chief, who was seated before a blazing log fire, with his back towards him as he entered. A second chair was placed beside the fire, and on the table close by stood flasks of wine and two handsome goblets.

The Captain turned round as our hero entered. Otho looked at him, almost doubting his identity, for, most assuredly, he was very unlike the robber of the morning. The dark hair, whiskers, and moustache had disappeared, which not only altered the appearance but even the age of the robber, so much so indeed that had Otho met him elsewhere he would assuredly not have recognised him. He wore the same fanciful costume, however, a close fitting dress, very much resembling the attire of a Tyrolese sharp-shooter, only profusely covered with small buttons, scarlet braid, and a crimson sash in place of a leather belt; but he had no weapons.

The brigand was apparently about six or seven and twenty years of age, and the expression of his countenance, without either whisker or moustache, was of a frank, careless, and somewhat jovial character ; but the most careful and determined disciple of Lavater could not detect in his physiognomy any indication of his infamous profession.

"My change of wig, whiskers, and moustache has, I see, Count, staggered you as to my personality," said the robber, politely handing him a chair; "you would not like to swear to my identity."

"No, not to your general appearance, but I could to your voice, which is somewhat remarkable."

"Ah! you are right there," said the brigand ; "my voice has before now nearly betrayed me. I have often tried to change it, but have never succeeded. How fares the Countess's fair daughter ?"

"I fancy," replied the Count, looking fixedly at the robber, "that you will find you have carried off a different person to the one you intended. The young lady is no relative whatever of the Countess di Sera."

The Captain looked surprised, but immediately said—

"Then upon my soul, I am very glad of it. How the mistake has arisen, I know not; but as you say such is the case, my comrades may be induced to demand a ransom within reason; for supposing her to be the Countess's daughter, the sum demanded for her release is enormous, in spite of all my efforts to the contrary. May I enquire, Count, who is the Signora, and how the change took place. Believe me in asking this, my desire is to serve you. I will explain why by and bye.''

"She is the daughter of a Corsican gentleman," answered the Count, " and was being educated in the same convent as the Countess di Sera's daughters, the youngest of whom was just recovering from a fever, and could not bear the journey, so her elder sister remained with her at the convent. The young lady you now detain was placed under the protection of the Countess, and was on her way to join her guardian at

Genoa, prior to proceeding to her home in Corsica. This is all the information I can give you."

" You will oblige me," said the brigand, " by asking the lady the name of her guardian, that we may at once negotiate with him concerning her release."

" You seemed to be aware," remarked Otho de Briesbach, " the evening I met you, of the coming of the Countess di Sera. The attack upon her carriage must have been premeditated."

" You are right, Count, it was. The adventure was undertaken chiefly by the captain of a larger force than mine, whose men generally inhabit the mountain passes between Aqui and Alessandria. He was at one time Captain of the entire band, but from some circumstances unnecessary to relate to you, we divided our forces. I remained here, and he went to the mountains of Aqui."

The Captain paused a moment or two, and then said in a very solemn tone—

"I wish, Count, I had never joined them at all. I don't pretend ever to have lived a strictly virtuous life, and I must confess that when I first united my fate to the brigands, I was not averse to the service, if carried on according to my system. But I ever had, and still have, an insuperable objection to shedding blood, but unfortunately I cannot always control my men, for there are many very ferocious, and with these I am anything but popular."

"Why not quit them," cried the Count, emphatically; "go to some other land—you are young—courageous; there is always a career open to a bold and willing spirit."

"Most gladly would I do so," said the Captain, "but I cannot. I am bound by a most solemn oath, which can only be absolved by the consent or breach of faith of those to whom the oath was given."

"Ought such oaths to be binding?" questioned Otho.

"All oaths, I think, should be binding," replied the Captain.

"Not, I think, if given under compulsion and fear," said the Count.

"Well, it may be so; but let me speak to you of events long since past—events that may cause you pain to hear, and, perhaps, induce you to look upon me with greater aversion and disgust than my present position warrants. Nevertheless, I will speak, for Providence alone has the right 'to visit the sins of the fathers upon the children,' and it is of our fathers I would now speak."

"Of our fathers!" repeated the Count, with a start, and a somewhat haughty tone; "what do you mean?"

There was an angry flash from the robber's eyes, and a flush upon his cheeks, and his lip trembled, as he replied in a still calm, mild tone,

"Have you any recollection of your boyhood? it was at that period you lost your father. He died from a wound received in a duel. My father perished from the same cause."

De Briesbach's astonishment was raised to a pitch almost of excitement; how his father's fate could have become known to the man before him, he could not conjecture: he, however, made no reply.

" Your father," continued the Captain, " was killed in a duel with an Italian of the name of Vachero."

" So I have been informed," said the Count. " I remember the name well ; but how this intelligence has reached your knowledge, I confess, greatly surprises me."

" Your surprise will cease, Count, when I tell you that the Julio Vachero, who unfortunately slew your father, was my own father !"

" Your father !" repeated the Count ; " you astonish me. Did you not say your father was also killed in a duel ?"

" Yes ; and so he was. The Count de Briesbach was mortally wounded and died in a few days. My father, though severely wounded, was still able to fly — for the

laws were very strict relative to duelling—
and with great difficulty reached Milan,
where my mother then resided.   His wound
rapidly grew worse, and he died in less than
a month after his return, bitterly lament-
ing having been forced into that unhappy
duel, for—" and the brigand spoke slowly
and emphatically—" for on his death-bed,
with a priest by his side, he declared he had
won the gold fairly and honourably from the
Count de Briesbach, who in a fit of passion
threw the dice in his face, and then struck
him.   I was a boy, at most fifteen or sixteen
years old at the time, but I heard the words,
and shall never forget them.   My mother is
still alive, and will vouch for what I say.
When I heard you give your name to the
Countess di Sera, the memory of the past,
and my father's death-bed, came as vividly
before me as if the occurrence had taken
place yesterday."

Otho de Briesbach heard the brigand to the
end without interruption, but with no little

surprise, and after a moment said thoughtfully, " Strange things occur in this world, and at strange times. I could never have anticipated this meeting with the son of Julio Vachero. It was from my uncle, the Baron de Newhoff, I first heard of my father's unfortunate fate. May I ask how it was that your mother and yourself were residing at Milan,and your father in Paris? My uncle mentioned that your father was an Italian adventurer, but did not name the part of Italy he came from."

The brigand's cheek flushed, but he replied, calmly,

" My father was by no means what is usually called an adventurer; he was by birth a native of Lucia, and possessed a good estate in the Ligurian territory. He was detected in a conspiracy to overthrow the detested tyranny of the rulers of Genoa, and his estates being confiscated, he fled with his wife and family. Afterwards, it cannot be denied, he chiefly suported himself by gambling. My mother did all she could to break him of so baneful a passion, which in the end gained complete mastery over him; but he was neither a sharper nor the associate of swindlers. His good fortune became so notorious that he quitted Milan and rambled through Germany and France, not staying long in any one place. It was during one of those wanderings that he unfortunately met your father in Paris, and both lost their lives in consequence."

A loud, shrill whistle sounded from without the cavern at that moment.

" That is for me," said the brigand. " I must bid you good-night, Count, as our messenger is returned from Campomarino. To-morrow I hope to be able to give you some intelligence with respect to our fair prisoner. You may rely upon my using my best endeavours to gain her release at a reasonable ransom. Marguerita will show you your place of rest, and there you will find your *valise*."

" Well," thought our hero, " this is turning out a most singular adventure; and I must

confess this bandit chief has some very remarkable traits in his character. Nevertheless, I wish I could see the Lady Vannina safe
out of the clutches of his band of villains."

Marguerita interrupted him in the midst
of his confused and perplexing thoughts by
offering to show him his couch, which was
within another branch of the caverns, and
by no means uncomfortable; its sides were
carefully matted, and the floor covered with a
kind of odoriferous broom. Of furniture
there was certainly a very scanty supply;
a chair, a table, and the couch, was all the
chamber contained, and across the entrance
was drawn a curtain of platted dried grass.

On the chair was his *valise*, unopened, and
as his own person had been free from the
hands of his captives, his purse, pistol, and
sword were still about him, and he placed
them carefully by his bedside, and without
undressing threw himself on his couch;
not that he expected to sleep, for with the
image of the beautiful Vannina floating before

his mind's eye, and the strangeness of his situation, he had quite enough to occupy his thoughts during the first night passed in the robber's cave.

CHAPTER X.

Otho passed the following day in the caverns chiefly in the society of the fair Vannina and the little girl Jaqueline. They saw no one save Marguerite, who prepared their meals for them. They passed out from the mouth of the cave, and seated on a projection of the rock, gazed down into the wild and extraordinary valley beneath.

"What a splendid, wild scene," cried Vannina, "and how impossible for any one to escape from this place without a guide. You see there is no possibility of getting either up or down from this small platform without the rope ladders."

" It assuredly is a singular stronghold,"
said the Count. " You said it reminded you
of your native mountains. I know but little
of Corsica, excepting its perpetual struggles
against the Republic of Genoa; but of the
country or its peculiarities I am ignorant;
but were I to judge of its natives by the fair
example before me, why—"

" Ah! Count," interrupted Vannina, with a
smile, " you must not use flattery to a wild
Corsican maiden, who knows little of the
world except by hearsay, my childhood having been passed amid the wild hills of Nonza,
and my girlhood within the gloomy walls of a
convent."

" Your young life has experienced early
misfortunes," said the Count, "though I trust
the present trial will be but short. The
robber Captain last night requested me to
obtain from you the name of your guardian—
your father, I presume, is in Corsica.'"

" Yes," returned Vannina; " he is in
Bastia; I hear the island is again disturbed.

Alas! for poor Corsica! the struggles to shake off a cruel yoke—but I beg pardon; I am what the good Countess di Sera calls a little rebel at heart, and cordially detest the very name of the Genoese, though my father and all his family connections and numerous vassals side with the Republic against what they call the rebellion of the islanders. I am not answering your question about my guardian. The fact is I have no guardian. My father entrusted me to the protection of a Corsican noble, also a friend to the Republic—the Count Domenico Rivalora, a relative of ours.

"I was to be educated in a convent, and as the Countess di Sera was desirous of placing her two daughters in the convent of St. Ursula, near Turin, the Count de Rivalora thought it advisable to place me under her protection. I soon learned to esteem her, and to love her two charming daughters. I have no doubt that the Count de Rivalora will find the sum these exacting brigands may demand.

My father is reputed very wealthy, and will not allow his only child to remain long a prisoner, when money only is required to release her."

The day wore away with our two young captives in a manner anything but tedious; in fact the Count never remembered the hours to have passed so rapidly. Love was insidiously marking them out as his captives. There appeared no doubt that the moment their captivity with the brigands should cease, their future lives would be influenced by the events of the last few days.

Otho de Briesbach was sitting immersed in thought by the fire, after Vannina had retired with little Jacqueline, to whom she had become much attached, for the child was extremely sensible, over serious for her years, and very interesting in her person and manner.

Marguerite had placed a flask or two of unexceptional wine before the Count, saying, "The Captain will be here shortly." And in less than ten minutes he entered the cave.

"I fear," said the Captain, saluting the Count, respectfully, "you have found the time tedious, notwithstanding you had the society of the Lady de Matrà, I am sorry to say I have no positive intelligence to impart to you."

The Count looked vexed and uneasy, saying—"What has happened? Do the lady's friends refuse to pay the ransom demanded, or are your demands so exorbitant as to require time to consider them?"

"I am sorry, Count, you are right in your suppositions. The sum demanded is preposterous—ruinous, even supposing the lady's father is as wealthy as he is represented to be. However, nothing certain is known yet; her friends are aware of the sum required for her release, but till to-morrow we cannot receive an answer. I did all in my power to make my comrades agree to accept easier terms, but my proposals were met with fierce reproach, and from Marco Remini and his gang with scorn and defiance.

"I will be candid with you, Count, for since I encountered you a singular change has come over me. I am disgusted with this brigand life. I demanded last night my release from my vows, declaring I was ready to take the required oaths, when a member quits the band, not to betray by word or deed our places of retreat, or our system of organisation, or any of the agents of the gang living in cities or towns. They refused to liberate me, and high words were the result, and only that the consequence to you and the lady might be serious, we had come to an open rupture."

The Count looked concerned at the prospect before him. He remained silent, for his thoughts were centered upon the Lady Vannina, for as regarded himself he felt perfectly indifferent. The captain filled his goblet with wine, and then said,

"There is no use, Count, in giving way to despondency. Keep up your spirits. I will not desert you or your charming *protegée*, and if to-morrow's answer is not to our mutual satisfaction, I have one way still left. If you are not inclined for sleep, I will give you a rapid outline of my life; it may beguile you from your sombre thoughts. What say you?"

"I shall gladly listen to you, for I do not feel the slightest inclination to sleep."

Helping himself to some wine, he allowed the Captain to commence his narrative, to which he might listen or not, as he felt inclined.

"I shall begin after my father's death, for I have nothing to say of myself till that event took place, except that I was a very wild and somewhat ungovernable boy, though devotedly attached to my poor mother, who took my father's death greatly to heart. She at once determined to return to Genoa, where she had several relations, hoping to do something for me through their interest.

"We reached Genoa without mishap, and as all danger from my father's political opinions and plots was at an end my mother's friends were willing to assist her. At Milan I regularly attended school, and at fourteen was tolerably well grounded in reading, writing, and book keeping, for my mother always hoped to be able to get me into a mercantile establishment. Accordingly, some short time after our arrival, I was placed in the counting-house of a very rich merchant, the Signor Matteo Gavotti.

" For several months I went on very well, but at the end of a year I began to find the confinement irksome. Signor Gavotti was a kind hearted man, and my mother, to whom I complained, spoke with the merchant, who very kindly promised to vary my employment, and I was sent in some of his vessels short voyages, as a clerk to his supercargo. I soon began to delight in this life—it suited me amazingly; and I acquitted myself so well, pleasing both the merchant and the supercargo, that the former promised, as soon as I was old enough, to send me out in one of his vessels as supercargo.

" Time rolled on, and though I committed several errors —was wild and heedless at times, —I still contrived to keep in the merchant's good graces. I was just twenty when he finished and launched a beautiful brig intended for the Odessa trade, which was then carried on with vigour by the Genoese merchants.

" The Signor Gavotti's family at this period consisted of three daughters and one son. The second daughter, Laurina, was a remarkably pretty girl, but became rather delicate as she advanced in life. She was at this period in her sixteenth year. I knew very little of the merchant's family, residing, as I did, entirely with my mother, and attending to my office business during the day. I met them occasionally on *fête* day, or birthdays; but sooth to say, I was treated somewhat haughtily by the son, a proud and imperious youth, and with easy politeness by the eldest daughter. Their mother had been dead many years.

" When the brig was launched, the merchant informed me she was to carry out a rich

cargo to the Black Sea, and return with corn
from Odessa, and that I should go out as her
supercargo. He was, he said, looking out for
a competent captain. I rejoiced at this, for I
enjoyed the sea and I also liked the kind of
life I had the power to lead during the periods
we remained in harbour.

"When the vessel was nearly ready for
sea Signor Gavotti informed me, in the course
of conversation, that his two eldest daughters
were going to spend the winter in Naples,
and that we were to land them, and the lady
to whose care they were to be entrusted,
at that city; and on our return voyage from
Odessa we were to touch at that port to
bring them home, for we should be detained
in the Black Sea four months, and he
thought a lengthened residence in Naples
would be of great benefit to Laurina.

"In three weeks the brig was laden and
ready for sea, but there was a difficulty about
the skipper; just in the nick of time, the
Signor Gavotti engaged one accustomed to

the navigation of the Black Sea. This skipper was a Sicilian, and brought most satisfactory letters from a wealthy mercantile house in Palermo. Accordingly Benedetto Lottero, the name of the Sicilian, was engaged. The skipper selected the crew, and all being ready for sailing, the ladies went on board. I was the last to go, for I received the final instructions, letters, papers, &c., for the various ports we were to touch at. Having taken an affectionate leave of my mother, I took a boat at Port del Mare and pulled out to the brig, which was lying at single anchor, her sails set and the men at the capstan, when I arrived alongside.

" 'Who the devil are you?' were the first words I heard, as I laid hold of a rope and gained the deck. I turned to the speaker, saying,

" 'Who do you suppose I am? The supercargo, of course!'

" 'Oh!' said the same rough voice. 'You are the supercargo, eh? Heave round, lads,

heave round,' and then turning round he sur-
veyed me from head to foot as leisurely as if
he had been examining the points of a horse.
' You are the supercargo, are you?' and he
laughed a coarse laugh. 'Where's your tom
cat to lick your chin, eh?'

"'If I had him,' I replied, in my turn
taking full measure of the huge bear before
me, 'besides licking my beard, he might be
useful to comb your whiskers, they look as if
they want a cat's claws.'

"'Stand by,' roared the skipper, without
heeding my words.

"' Aye! aye! sir,' sung out the sailors.

"'Brace round the yards,' and round they
went, filling to the fine *tramontane* that was
then blowing out of the harbour.

" The brig rapidly gathered way, and
gliding between the two gigantic moles, that
form the harbour of Genoa, stood away for
the open sea. During this operation I was
taking a careful survey of the skipper, whose
singular reception considerably nettled me.

In stature he was below the middle height, but I never before beheld so vast a breadth of chest and back, supported on limbs that looked like pillars. He appeared about forty-five years of age, with a round bullet head, small but fiery dark eyes, a thick grisly head of hair, and a pair of shaggy whiskers, that appeared to have never come in contact with comb or brush, encircling his throat, and covering the entire sides of his face; altogether I never beheld so unpromising a looking skipper. He was the personification of a ferocious buccaneer. He did not come near me again, so I went down below to stow away my papers and to enquire if the ladies—who I found in the handsome cabin, busily arranging their baggage—wanted anything.

" ' What a rough creature my father has selected for a captain,' said the eldest of my master's daughters; ' he appears a perfect sea monster. We heard him address you, when you came on board. Was that the first time you had seen him ?'

"'The very first time,' I replied, laughing, 'and it would give me no pain if the introduction were never renewed.'

"'He quite startled me,' said Laurina, 'for he stood staring at me with his fiery eyes when we came upon deck, and instead of civilly handing us on board, or showing us the way to the cabin, he muttered "a cursed troublesome lot—put me out of my course—that sickly thing will die if we get rough weather.'"

"'Yes, a most uncomplimentary brute,' said the elder sister, laughing heartily, as Laurina mimicked the skipper. 'Thank heaven! three days with this wind and we shall get rid of this sea savage.'

"'But you, Signor Vachero,' put in Laurina, 'will have a horrid time of it with him.'

"'Oh! I don't trouble my head about his want of civility. Our pursuits will be very different.'

"Having seen that all the ladies required

was at hand, I returned to the small cabin allotted to me, and settled and packed away my letters and papers. After that I returned to the deck to see how things got on there, and to inspect our crew.

" When I stood upon deck I perceived our Hercules of a skipper standing close by the tiller, with a telescope in his hand, looking towards the shore. To my extreme astonishment the sails of the brig were braced sharp up, with the vessel's head right for the bluff headland of Monte Porte Finico. Now as our course for Naples was due south, and the wind was right aft, I thought it a very extraordinary circumstance to see the brig close hauled, standing in for the land.

. " I considered it my duty to enquire the reason for so strange a proceeding ; and walking up to the skipper, who, stood with his huge limbs widely apart, eying me ferociously, as I approached.

" ' Beg pardon, skipper,' I said, speaking quite civilly, ' anything wrong, anything forgotten, that we are standing in for the land and losing this fine breeze?'

" 'Who the devil gave you leave to ask questions?' literally roared the brute. 'Keep a civil tongue in your jaws, youngster, or you'll get the slack of a rope where you'd little like to feel it.'

" Young as I was I never allowed myself to be cowed, or bullied, by any of the captains I sailed with. I was aware that, in many instances, supercargos were hated by the skippers of merchant vessels, but such a brute as this I had never before encountered. I felt my face turn scarlet at the man's gross language, and replied,

" 'Do not imagine, man, because you have the body of a bear and the voice of a bull, that I will tolerate your insolence, perfectly uncalled for as it is. I say again, you are not doing that which is right; you are not pursuing the right course.'

" At first I thought he intended knocking

me down with the telescope, but all of a
sudden he burst into an immoderate fit of
laughter; so violent was it that I almost ap-
prehended he would be seized with an apo-
plectic fit, and seeing a bucket of water close
by my side, I grasped hold of the handle, intending to give him its contents, but he called
out in time.

"'Avast there! avast! stay your hand.
Upon my soul you nearly killed me : you so
put me in mind of a bantam strutting up to a
full grown cock.   There, don't colour up in
the gills like a cock turkey courting.   By the
devil's beard you'll be the death of me!'

"I never felt more exasperated in my life;
I did not know what to make of the man. As
to any personal encounter with him, it was out
of the question, and it would only end in his
putting me in irons for mutiny.   When the
skipper had done laughing, he turned coolly
to the man at the helm, saying,

"'Keep her away a point or so—that's the

boat,' and he lifted his telescope to his eye and looked steadily at a dark object apparently about a mile ahead.

" I thought it better to swallow my passion, as it could lead to no good result, and therefore walked forward to see what kind of men our crew were. Leaning over the weather-bow were four stout, able-bodied seamen; two others were employed coiling away the cable, and two down below. The men leaning over the bulwarks looked up as I came near them, and certainly, as far as looks went, they were not more engaging than the skipper ; they were all young, hard-featured men, wild and reckless, and looking remarkably bronzed, even for Italians.

" 'I will try,' I said, mentally, 'if they are more courteous or civil than their skipper.' I addressed them, saying, 'What is that object ahead, my men, that we seem to be steering for?'

" ' Why, can't you use your eyes, lad,' said one of the men ; 'they are young enough.'

"'They want squabbing out with a wet mop,' said another, laughing, 'if he can't make out the difference atween a ship's boat and a porpoise.'

"'Then, it's a boat we are steering for,' I quietly observed, looking at the object, which I now clearly saw was a boat full of men. I was startled. What on earth could our captain mean? There was something very alarming in his manner of proceeding. We rapidly approached the boat, which had a signal hoisted; I could easily see that it contained fifteen men. It was a long, narrow craft, very like those used in whale fishing.

"While I stood anxiously watching, the voice of the skipper was again heard shouting out, 'Fore-topsail there!' The helm was instantly put down, and the brig shot up in the wind; her topsails were hauled to windward, and the brig became stationary. The next instant the boat, full of men, was pulled rapidly alongside.

" I was walking aft, thoroughly astonished, when I encountered the skipper coming towards me. He looked me full in the face for a moment or two, and then, taking hold of one of my arms, said, in a low, distinct tone,

" ' Young man, listen to me : I don't wish to hurt you, for I think you will turn out useful to me. Go down below, and shut your eyes on what is going on. This brig is now mine' (I felt his hand grasp me like a vice) ; ' let you be ever so true to your master, you can do nothing. Go down quietly, and assure the women they shall come to no hurt, for I will land them and their baggage somewhere on the coast of Corsica.'

" Without another word, he almost forced me down the cabin stairs, closed the hatch and bolted it. I was then only a slight youth of twenty, with some promise of the strength I afterwards acquired, and which you see I now possess. I had spirit enough, but you will admit I was unable to do anything in such an extraordinary case of downright piracy, within fifteen miles of the port of Genoa. I stood for several minutes, confounded, on the stairs, scarcely knowing whether I was awake or in a dream.

CHAPTER XI.

"I WAS powerless to defeat this man's piratical intentions. The whole affair, must have been systematically planned long before his presenting himself to the Signor Gavotti as a skipper to the brig. Most likely the letters of recommendation from the mercantile house at Palermo were all forgeries.

"I heard, as I stood deliberating how I should break the intelligence to the merchant's daughters, the tramp of many feet upon the deck, and the loud and never-to-be-forgotten laugh of the skipper. I knew now there was

ı 5

no use in hesitating, therefore instantly entered the cabin, where the ladies were still occupied in arranging their attire, quite unconscious of the event that would certainly change their destination, if nothing worse should occur.

" 'Well, signor Vachero,' said Laurina, looking up as I entered, she was employed emptying a trunk, 'is there anything wrong upon deck, for we heard a great noise overhead? I suppose nothing unusual, for the vessel is so steady that I can scarcely fancy we are out at sea.'

" 'I fear—I fear—I shall greatly disturb your minds, though I trust—I feel almost satisfied the brute will keep his word.'

" The ladies stared at me, with evident astonishment, as I began this confused kind of speech.

" 'What is it that disturbs you, signor Vachero?' asked the elder of the two sisters, 'You appear agitated.   Has this rough captain again been behaving rudely to you?'

" ' Your father has been deceived, signora. The skipper is neither more nor less than a buccaneer. He has taken on board fifteen or sixteen rough looking men off Porte Fino; and not five minutes since, he told me very coolly that the brig was his; at the same time telling me to let you know that he intended you no harm, and would land you on the coast of Corsica.'

" I need scarcely say that I did not get through this recital without sundry ejaculations and emotions of terror from the ladies.

" ' What is to be done?' cried the elder daughter. ' The Saints preserve us! should this pirate forfeit his word, what will become of us? What is he going to do with the vessel?'

" ' Holy Virgin!" exclaimed the lady who had charge of the young girls, and who cer· tainly was very much the wrong side of forty. ' Holy Virgin! perhaps he intends selling us as concubines to the Grand Turk.'

"Laurina, however, was the least agitated of the three. She looked paler than usual, but not much frightened. My eyes rested on hers, and then, for the first time, I felt that she was dearer to me than I had imagined. After a time I succeeded in somewhat calming the worst of their fears; and in my endeavour Laurina aided me, and showed more firmness and good sense under misfortune than either her sister or the signora.

"'If this captain keeps his word,' said Laurina, 'and from what you say, I really think he will, and lands us anywhere in Corsica, we shall suffer but little inconvenience, as we can easily return thence to Genoa. Did he say you were to land with us, Signor Vachero?' And the girl looked at me, I flattered myself, a little anxiously.'

"'Of that, I confess I am doubtful,' I replied.

"'Good Heaven!' she exclaimed; 'he surely does not think of forcing you to become a pirate.'

"'If he thinks to do so,' I said, 'he will be mistaken. The brig is again under way, I perceive, by the motion. I will see if the skipper has unfastened the hatch, and whether he intends to keep us captives.'

"I left the matron in a most piteous state of alarm, fancying herself already established in the harem of either the Grand Turk or the Dey of Algiers.

"When I pushed at the hatch over the cabin stairs, it readily fell back, and I as-ascended to the deck. The first person I encountered was the skipper, who was walking up and down, and faced me as I popped my head up.

"'Well, my lad, how's the wind with the women? blows a hurricane, or a gentle sou' wester, eh?'

"I was completely nonplussed by the perfect coolness of the man. In fact, I scarcely knew how to answer him.

"'Why, youngster, you seem struck all of a heap,' he continued. 'You couldn't look

worse if you were expecting to be run up to
the yard arm. Cheer up, my fine fellow;
there's a nice life before you. Get the women
ashore as soon as possible, for between you
and me—' and he gave me a poke in the
ribs with the end of his telescope, that nearly
broke them—' there's no trusting a ship's
company with a couple of handsome girls
before their eyes. Besides, I don't—no, curse
it, I ain't so bad as that neither—I don't want
to rob the old man of his girls as well as his
brig.'

"'Then you really intend putting them
ashore?' I anxiously demanded, clutching
him by the arm.

"'There's my hand to it,' he exclaimed.
'I'm cursed if I don't.''

"I very foolishly trusted my hand to the
mercy of his, by way of ratifying the contract,
and he pressed my unfortunate fingers so
energetically, that I almost roared with the
pain.

"'When?' I asked, as soon as I regained

my breath, after his affectionate squeeze.
'When do you think you can put us ashore ?'

"'Us !' cried the skipper, with one of his
boisterous laughs; 'us! who the devil's us?
You don't surely think I am going to part
with my supercargo, ha ! ha! ha!'—and he
got red in the face with the hoarse laugh
in which he indulged. 'No, no, my lad,
I'm getting fond of you. I mean to
make a man of you, and teach you to steer,
point, and reef. What a jolly life we shall
lead. You don't know what's before you.
There now, don't open your jaws again till
cook has given you something to put in them,
so just go forward and order the fellow to get
supper or dinner for the women, and beg they
will excuse my joining them. Make the most
of them, my lad, for by this time to-morrow
we shall bid them farewell.'

"And off he walked, leaving me to my own
reflections, and not a little bewildered and
very much vexed.

"I passed an hour to two with the merchant's family, talking over the strange event that had taken place; but the wind having freshened, the motion of the vessel as she gained the open sea increased so much as to produce symptoms of sea-sickness, and forced the ladies to retire to their berths, and I went to rest at a late hour. I could not sleep for a long time, but tossed and turned and tormented myself with plans and projects impossible of execution.

" Towards morning, however, I fell asleep, worn out with my own thoughts. How long I slept I could not tell, but it was broad day when I awoke, and I could perceive by the motion that the vessel was still under canvass. I jumped hastily up and threw on my coat, the only garment I had taken off, and proceeded to open my door, which, to my consternation, I found fastened. The noise I made trying to open it, brought some one, for I heard the bolt drawn back and the door opened, and standing, with a broad grin on his red face, just outside was the skipper.'

" 'Well, my lad, you have made a fine sleep of it. I landed the women two hours ago, but if you make haste you will catch a glimpse of Cape Corsica.'

" 'Landed the women!' I exclaimed, confounded, and in fact stupified. 'Why fasten me in—why let me sleep ?'

" ' Sleep! there's nothing so refreshing as a sound sleep,' and the skipper laughed; ' you slept like a prince. The women, sweet dears, went away like lambs. The young one cried a bit, and told me to take care of you. I suppose she meant I was to rear you tenderly, and teach you to walk in the right path. She wishes you to sail always over smooth water,' and again he laughed boisterously and ascended on deck, leaving me to follow.

" Bursting with rage and vexation, I went on deck. I cast my eyes around, and beheld the bold coast of Corsica astern of us, some six or eight miles. The brig was under every stitch of canvass she could set, with a fine breeze from the north east. Some eight or ten rough-looking sailors were sitting in a group by the foremast, the sun shone bright and glorious, and the water sparkled and rippled and broke into foaming billows under our bows as the brig plunged rapidly through them. All looked bright and cheerful, but my own heart, that in truth felt heavy and oppressed.

"As I walked to and fro, I determined in my own mind to say no more to our skipper, but let him inform me of his own accord what his plans were with respect to me. I was young—very young, Count de Briesbach, and as I said before, somewhat wild and thoughtless, and when in Genoa, kept but indifferent associates. Nevertheless, I had committed no act deserving a worse name than indiscreet.'"

"I was naturally of a buoyant spirit—ex-

tremely fond of the sea—had heard of the
exploits of the buccaneers, and I thought 'if
this skipper is a buccaneer, and intend
taking the brig out into those seas, I should
have no objection to such a life.' The com·
mon pirate or *ladri di'mare* I considered quite
a different thing.

" I was left entirely to myself the whole
day. I did not address any of the sailors
who went to and fro, and as I passed near
the binnacle, I took a look to see what
course we were steering. The brig was going
away south and by west, which I conjectured
would bring us close up with the Barbary
coast."

" ' Does the skipper intend selling the cargo
and craft?' was the first question I
asked myself. I was saved the trouble of
much thinking, for in the midst of my doubt
the captain came up to me, saying, and slap-
ping me familiarly on the shoulders at the
same time—

"'Come, my lad—come to dinner; fine breeze—she walks, eh?. A real clipper. I knew she would prove one the moment I set eyes on her. Come, bear a hand ; I want to have some palaver with you.'

"I sat down to a very good dinner with the skipper and a stout, fine looking man, of about three or four and thirty. There was very little conversation carried on, for the skipper and his lieutenant—for such he called him—seemed to me as if eating for a wager. As soon as the lieutenant had emptied a can of wine, holding about three pints, he walked away, leaving me with the skipper, who kept at his work ten minutes longer, at least, and at length ended by following the example of his lieutenant in drinking a share of wine.

"'Now, my lad, let us talk a bit. I'm all the better for my dinner—how are you, eh? Now I daresay,' he continued, without heeding whether I replied or not, 'you take me for a regular cut-throat, a ferocious, blood-thirsty pirate, eh? Don't you, my lad?'

" ' Well, something very like it,' I replied.

" ' Ha ! good; so I thought,' he returned, not speaking in the least angrily. ' Yes, I have a ferocious look—it suits my profession. Quite impossible to get on without a down-right bloodthirsty countenance. It serves to keep the crew in order, and it settles small matters without blows. But I tell you what, my lad, I'm as tender-hearted as a chicken."

" I felt very much inclined to laugh, and the skipper saw it.

" ' I'm curs'd if I ain't,' he repeated ; 'listen now, while I tell you how I came to take this brig. But stop—you take us all for a set of villanous pirates, don't you ?'

" ' Why, what on earth else could I take you for, ?' I replied, quietly, ' after what I have witnessed.'

" 'All right and above board, my lad; but you're wrong in your reckoning. We are

none of us pirates, nor don't intend being
pirates. No, blow me high and dry, if I'm
not telling you the truth. Just take a couple
of bottles out of that locker you're sitting on;
this talking is such cursed dry work. That's
right, lad—now listen.

"'The Signor Matteo Gavotti, the wealthy
German merchant, owed the Signor Perugia
Malatesta, a merchant of Palermo, the large
balance of a long, unsettled account. The
Signor Malatesta died, and left his property,
settled and unsettled, to his younger brother,
the Signor Luigi Malatesta.—Cursed dry
work this, my lad; come, whet your whistle.
Well, then, Luigi Malatesta did all he could
to get the Genoese merchant to settle his
claims. The proper vouchers were wanted,
so he refused till they were produced—blow
him! he had them himself.'

"I stared at the skipper; I thought he
was either getting drunk or insane.

"'Yes, my lad. First—Luigi Malatesta

swore he would have the sum or an equivalent.
I'm Luigi Malatesta—and curse him ! I've got
the brig and the cargo ; they will nearly
balance the debt. Now, my lad, what do
you think of all this ?' And the skipper
looked at me with his fierce dark eyes.

"' Why,' I replied, ' I think it is all very
strange. But how did you contrive to deceive the Signor Gavotti, so as to induce him
to entrust you—a total stranger—with the
command of this fine brig and valuable
cargo ?'

"' Well, my lad, that was partly good
luck ; you see, when I found the Signor Gavotti obstinately refusing to settle my claims,
I determined to have a trip to Genoa and
see what I could do in person. I have passed
fifteen years of my life cruising in the Spanish
main, along with some of the old buccaneers.
I was at Providence when Governor Rodgers
arrived there with two men-of-war. We
were employed, you see, fishing up the silver

from the wrecks of the galleons in the Gulf of Florida.

"'I was at the time lieutenant to one Captain Vane, a noted buccaneer; but this Commodore or Governor Rodgers swore we were all a set of cut-throat pirates, and wanted to hang my captain and all his crew. No go that, my lad; I never admired the hempen cravat, so we slipped our cables, set fire to a prize we had, hoisted our colours, fired at one of the men-of-war, and sailed away from the coast.'

"'Why, then, Captain,' I interrupted, while the skipper, who seemed fond of talking of the past, was helping himself to copious draughts of wine, 'you have been a pirate.'

"He looked rather fierce at first, and I began to repent my expression; but he only laughed rather grimly, saying, with an oath,

"'Pirate! who says the cruisers or bucca- neers of the Spanish Main are pirates? No such thing, my lad. We only cruised against the Spaniards; however, that's neither here nor there. I sailed with Vane, and was getting rich, when our crew mutinied, and Captain Vane and myself and four others were put into a small sloop, with a scanty store of provisions and sent adrift; but would you believe it? the villains didn't let us have even a can of wine.

" ' We met with many adventures and more distress, which made Vane so desperate that he became bloodthirsty and cruel, and we separated. He put me ashore on a small uninhabited island, near the Bay of Honduras; and there I lived, in the best way I could, until a ship put in there from Jamaica, commanded by an old buccaneer, named Holford. I had sailed with him before, and he willingly took me on board. He swore that if he caught Vane, he would hang him, and so he did.

" ' I remained with Holford till he returned with his ship to Jamaica; and then, being tired of the roving life I had led for years, which left me as poor at the end as I was at the beginning, I shipped for Europe.

"'When I arrived at Palermo, I found my brother—the only one of my family left—. had, in the course of years, become a rich merchant. I don't know how it was, whether I brought him ill luck or not, but in five years after my return, he became nearly bankrupt, and died of vexation, leaving me the wreck of his property. So there, my lad, I have spun you a long yarn about myself.'

"'You have, Captain; but you began to tell me how you got possession of the brig, and finished by getting to Providence, Honduras, and Heaven knows where besides.'

"'Ha! so I did, my lad; but you see I wanted to give you an idea of how I passed my youth. Not very profitably you see, as far as getting rich; but never mind, we'll make it up now. We'll cruise in the Spanish Main with a craft of our own.'

"'And get suspended from the yard-arm of

some Government cruiser, eh, Captain ? like your worthy commander Vane,' I replied.

" ' No such thing, my lad. Vane became a blood-thirsty pirate, and stuck at nothing. We will cruise under a fair letter of marque from the Government. But come, heave a hand. I am as dry as a red herring with talking; can't spin any more yarns now. Take a turn on deck, and after supper I'll tell you how I got the brig.'

CHAPTER XII.

" I had a long conversation with our skipper after supper, and in his rambling style I became acquainted with the manner in which he contrived to deceive the Signor Gavotti, and also with his plans for the future. He had sailed from Palermo with an old pilot captain well acquainted with the navigation of the Black Sea. This captain was on his voyage to apply for the command of the brig, and carried letters of recommendation from several ship owners. During the cruise the two skippers became very intimate. In a heavy gale, the foreyard snapped across, and unfortunately struck Captain Lotero on the head and fractured his skull ; he died three days after, leaving his papers and few effects in the care of Luigi Malatesta. The vessel was bound for Leghorn, and there the unfortunate skipper was buried, under the direction of Malatesta, who immediately after proceeded to Genoa.

" During this short voyage he planned his scheme of passing himself off as the Captain Lotero, whose papers he possessed, and being a stranger to every one in Genoa, he easily succeeded in obtaining the command of the brig. Having accomplished thus much, his next step was to engage a crew. For this purpose he went to Porto Fino, a place notorious for its nest of smugglers and a bold race of seamen. After a good deal of manœuvring, he engaged fifteen able-bodied men to join him. His intention was, in the first place, to run the brig to Tangiers, dispose of her cargo, purchase arms and ammunition, and then shape his course for Providence, where he could arm his vessel and increase his crew.

"The first use he intended making of me, was to compel me to forge papers, proving his right and title to the brig, and all she contained, and after having accomplished this, I was to become his second lieutenant— his first having been already provided. I heard all his plans without uttering a single word, and he made no remark on my silence. Within the space of twenty-four hours all his intentions and our destinies were changed.

"The following day we were bowling along under a press of sail, fine breeze, and fair weather, when the man aloft sung out that there was a large lateen-rigged craft, close-hauled, standing across our course. We could see there was a vessel ahead, but her rig was not distinguishable. We were going nine knots through the water, and in little more than half-an-hour we could make her out distinctly. She was a long, low craft— much longer than the brig, under three immense lateen sails.

" ' Take in studden sail,' said the skipper, who was attentively examining the stranger through his glass. ' That fellow is either a Spanish *guarda costa* or a Salee pirate. He has just tacked. Keep her away a couple of points more westerly. She evidently intends speaking us. What arms have we got below?' demanded the skipper of his lieutenant.

" Our men were all on deck ; we numbered eight-and-twenty.

" ' Only a dozen muskets and a lot of boarding pikes,' answered the lieutenant.

" ' If we can't beat her in sailing,' muttered the skipper, with an oath, ' for curse her ! she's a pirate—her decks are crowded with men—and by heaven ! she's tacked. Keep her two points more to the westward, and take a haul at the braces. It's no use fighting; but by all that's blue, we'll do something. Heave everything in the shape of iron and lead you can lay hold of into those two miserable-looking ten-pounders—curse 'em! I'll try and send some of those yellow devils to the infernal regions before I part with the brig.'

" I began to look around me with great anxiety, for at my age the prospect of a life of slavery in the foreground was anything but pleasant. I much preferred the chance of being knocked on the head, so I ran down below and armed myself with a brace of pistols of my own, and an old cutlass.

" ' When I again went on deck it was very evident that we were pursued by a pirate, for just as I turned to look how we stood, a wreath of smoke curled from the deck of the stranger, and the report of a large cannon boomed over the water."

" ' Curse him!' growled our skipper;

'that's out of an infernal swivel gun, and by my soul, a big one too, for the ball was scarcely fifty yards from us.'

" We were gradually getting close hauled, hoping, after a time, to be so situated as to get before the wind—the brig's best point of sailing. We could not do so, until we brought our enemy in the same position as ourselves. We were all anxiously watching the rover. We caught a glimpse of her flag; it was the pirate flag with a vengeance—a black one, with the skull and cross bones. The skipper made this out easy enough with his glass, and showered a profusion of oaths upon the pirates and their fathers for six generations back.

"The vessel gained on us rapidly; we could see that plainly enough, and every instant we expected another shot from her immense swivel gun, which we could now make out worked upon a circle between her fore and main masts. A wreath of snow-white vapour

warned us to look out, and the next instant was
heard the rush of the ball as it passed between
our masts, cutting away our weather braces
and knocking our booms to splinters.   We
left them out to be ready.

"'Square away, my lads,' roared the skipper; 'now's our time—run up everything—
confound her, she's got the legs of us on a
wind, anyhow.'

"In a few minutes we were dead before
the wind, and covered with a cloud of canvas.
Up went the helm of the pirate, and throwing
her enormous lateen sails (what sailors term
wing on wing), she looked like some flying
monster of the deep pursuing its prey.   We
watched our pursuer with the greatest possible
anxiety ; half-an-hour passed, and the skipper swore she didn't gain an inch.   Another
half-hour passed anxiously, and the wind
began to fall.   Suddenly the lower part of the
foresail of the pirate was brailed, and again
the swivel sent forth its deadly contents. The

sea being remarkably smooth, the aim of the pirates was uncommonly accurate. This time the shot struck the brig right in the stern, smashing the window frames, knocking our cabin bulk-head to atoms, and completely lodging itself in the cargo.

" Ten minutes after, a more destructive shot struck our main gaff, carried away part of our cross-trees and badly splintered the main yard. Down came our main-sail, and away flew our main-top-sail, while the studden sails fluttered about in ribbons. Our skipper remained perfectly cool, though he muttered and swore fearfully. Considering the number of our hands, we repaired these disasters tolerably quickly; but the pirate evidently gained upon us, and another shot bringing down our main top-mast, with all its load of canvas, laid us completely at the mercy of our pursuers.

" 'I tell you what, lads,' said our skipper, tossing off a can of brandy, and handing round a jar of the same spirit, ' let us 'die game! Haul those guns the same side— heave to, and when the bloody pirates come alongside to board us, slap their whole contents into their cursed carcasses.'

" These orders were obeyed; the men seemed to be imbued with the same spirit of vengeance and rage as the skipper. As to myself, I felt singularly uncomfortable, for certainly after getting the dose from our two guns, it was no great stretch of imagination to suppose the pirates would massacre us without mercy. Our men had first of all hoisted out the long boat and thrown into it oars and sundry articles, thinking to make use of it and desert the brig, but before doing so, they resolved to have another slap at the pirates, as our skipper expressed it.

" The brig was almost motionless on the water, the sun was nearly down, and the wind rapidly dying away. The pirate was within pistol shot, and we could see that they numbered nearly eighty or a hundred turbaned followers of Mahomet. She was a Salee rover; brailing her huge main-sail, she shot up right alongside—her deck one mass of swarthy pirates, eagerly thirsting to mount our side. At that moment the two guns were brought to bear upon the crowd, the skipper himself, with a savage curse, applying the match, and instantaneously they poured their deadly contents into the thickly-wedged mass of pirates preparing to board.

" The effect was terrible; one gun burst, so rammed had it been with implements of destruction. A hideous yell followed the discharge, and the deck of the pirate was covered with the dead and dying—a great many being most horribly mutilated.

" Had our brig been in a condition to carry sail, we might probably have got away, but we were too disabled and the wind too light. The next minute we were boarded with fearful yells and hideous imprecations. I, however, slipt over the side and swam to the long boat which was adrift, some twenty yards astern. I got safely in, and flung myself flat along the bottom. I had scarcely done so, when a report, which caused even the boat I was in to heave and rock as if tossed by a storm, induced me to jump up. What was my astonishment and horror when I perceived a vast volume of smoke and flame surrounding the spot where the pirate and brig were, and hurled through the air I beheld blackened timbers and scattered limbs of human beings whirling and turning with great rapidity. I gazed upon the scene like one bewildered. My hair seemed to stand on end, with horror, as dismembered bodies fell with a splash into the sea around me.

" As the vast volume of smoke cleared away, I beheld the brig still floating, her foremast and yards standing, but the mainmast and its gear were hanging over the side, and one side her bulwarks were torn from their stanchions; but of the pirate xebecque, not a vestige was to be seen, except broken spars and rent timbers.

" I could perceive several figures climbing the side of the brig, some swimming towards her, and a few coming down the rigging of the foremast.

" ' Thus,' thought I, ' have perished the plans and projects of Luigi Malatesta ; a short hour ago, master of a fine brig and rich cargo; and now, perhaps, a mutilated corpse.'

" The shades of night were fast creeping over the ocean—not a breath of wind disturbed its gently heaving bosom ; but it appeared to me, to judge by the thick gloom that was spreading over the sky, that before morning there would be plenty of wind. I was alone, the shadow of night enshrouded the brig from my sight, and I felt an overpowering melancholy, from which I strove to rouse myself.

"I overhauled the articles in the boat; they consisted of masts, sails, and oars, and that was all. She was a large fine boat, with the owner's name and the name of the brig painted in large letters in the inside of her stern. I was wet and cold, though the season of the year was spring. I doubted being able to step the mast, which was a heavy one, the oars were only to be worked singly, and I had but a very faint idea which way to steer to reach the nearest coast. The Spanish coast, I judged, lay away to the westward about a hundred and fifty miles; but my chief hope lay in being picked up by some passing craft.

"I placed one of the oars out over the side, shipped the rudder, and holding by the tiller with one hand, propelled the boat easily through the water, for exercise and to warm my limbs. It was an exceedingly dark night, neither moon nor starlight to enable me to judge which way I was steering. However, the exertion warmed me, and I continued for nearly an hour, when suddenly a huge black object rose before me. I was on the point of calling out, when I at once, by its solitary foremast, recognised the brig. I quietly put by my oar and listened. Not a sound reached my ear, save the creaking of the unbraced yards and the flap of the heavy canvas, as it struck against the masts, with the gentle motion of the vessel, but not a sound of the human voice could be heard.

" A strange desire to board the brig came over me, notwithstanding the risk I ran, should any of the pirates be upon deck. I judged, however, they would be below, most probably drunk, although they were followers of the false prophet, for I knew there was a large quantity of brandy and Hollands in the brig.

" I listened for some minutes; not a sound could be heard. I fastened the boat to the ropes of the mainmast, that hung with the rigging over the side, and without any difficulty gained the deck. I paused, rather startled, for a faint light came up the companion stairs; part of the cabin skylight was broken and a light shone up through the glass, whilst a murmur of voices reached my ears from below.

" My first thought was to slide down the side again, but intense curiosity caused me to creep on my knees and hands to the hole in the sky-light, whence cautiously I looked down through the glass. There were the pirates sure enough. I could count seventeen of them ; and there were others wounded and bruised, I imagined, stowed away in the berths. A more horrid set of wretches I never beheld. The large table of the cabin was covered with jars of spirits and all kinds of eatables, taken from the broken lockers. Some of the men had their faces grimed with powder, and blood smeared all over. Others had their heads bound up—three or four were drinking and smoking—one or two stretched on the floor—and five or six earnestly conversing.

"They were all Moors. I turned away from the horrible sight and got down the side into the boat and pushed it round to the bows. I again fastened her and climbed up on the brig's fore deck, hoping to get down into the sailors' cabin and obtain some biscuits and water. As I stole quietly across the deck, I frequently paused to listen, thinking every sound I heard was that of a pirate ascending the companion stairs.

CHAPTER XIII.

"In my progress from the bows of the brig towards the fore cabin, I put my foot upon sundry articles strewn over the deck; a large pea-coat I most joyfully appropriated to myself. Just as I reached the entrance to the cabin, I heard a deep groan and a smothered exclamation as of agony and rage.

"I paused; it was intensely dark. I listened; I was not mistaken. I heard the groan repeated, quite close to me. In my passage along the deck I nearly fell over two dead bodies. I shuddered and pur-

sued my way. A little further on I perceived, through the uncertain light, a most
appalling sight; from the fore yard, which
was braced sharp round, seven bodies were
suspended by the legs. They all nearly
touched the deck; but another body, also
hanging in the same manner, either
through its fierce struggles or the rope slip-
ping, lay with its head and shoulders resting
upon the deck. From this body came the
groans ; the rest had evidently been long
dead. I stooped, and with a start, recognised
Luigi Malatesta, the unfortunate skipper.
He was alive perfectly sensible, and recognised me at once as I bent over him. Con-
scious of our critical situation, he said in a
low voice,

"'Ha! lad, this is a nice fix, isn't it? Cut
away—cut away, my lad; ¡curse the villains!
their rope has cut to the bone.'

"Fortunately I had my knife, and instantly
cut the cord that bound his hands, and then,

though not without difficulty, those that held him by the legs, letting him down as softly as possible. All this time I trembled, lest some of the pirates should come upon deck ; but fortunately all remained quiet.

" It was some minutes ere the skipper could stand. His immense strength, great perseverance, and fearful struggles had saved his life. He had worked with such vigour that he had hauled the rope over the yard sufficiently to rest his shoulders on the deck. Nevertheless, had I not visited the brig, he would only have increased his torments.

" While he was gaining strength to stand I explained to him how I came there. He rubbed his hands violently, as he swore deadly oaths he would have a desperate revenge. He very soon gained the use of his legs, saying to me—

" ' Go down, lad, into the boat and stand by ; I will descend to the fore cabin for a bag of biscuit and a flask of wine. There is a small keg of water close to the hatch; I saw the reptiles drinking from it; take it into the boat with you.'

"I told him I thought he had better go down into the boat and let me go into the fore cabin.

" 'No, no, my lad, leave that to me; I know exactly where the things are stowed. Come, bear a hand with the water.' I found the keg, which contained six gallons; I lowered it with a rope, and then followed and stowed it away. It was some time before Luigi made his appearance, so long, indeed, that I was on the point of again going on deck to ascertain the cause of his long delay, when he hailed me in a low voice, and handed down a bag of biscuit and a jar of spirits; but he had not been able to find any wine. He then slung himself down the side, and in an excited tone told me to push off as quickly as possible, as he was done up, and must lie down, but would hold the tiller while I pulled an oar.

" He swore all the blood in his body had got into his head, and made him top-heavy. I certainly thought the position in which I found him was quite enough to do that. I pulled away with one oar for about ten minutes, when I was startled by seeing a bright light suddenly illumining the darkness that surrounded us.

" ' There it is—there it is,' roared my companion, in a voice that startled me. ' All right, my lad, curse the swarthy reptiles; I have done more for them than they did for me. They have the choice of fire or water ; ha ! ha ! ha ! curse them !'

" I gazed in astonishment ; the flame grew brighter and brighter ; the entire bow of the brig was now a sheet of fire, which was eagerly and rapidly rushing up the rigging of the foremast. We could see the dark figures of the pirates as they rushed up on the deck.

" ' Good heavens ! you have set the brig on fire,' I exclaimed.

" 'Aye, lad; and a fire the swarthy devils will

never quench ; curse them. I struck a light in the fore-cabin. I knew where to find the tinder-box. Ha! ha! ha! You are too tender-hearted, my lad; so I didn't tell you what I intended doing. I broke open a locker full of jars of oil, and poured out their contents in every direction. The bulkhead was full of log-wood shavings. I saturated them with oil just before leaving the vessel. I ignited the log-wood, and the swarthy brutes are now enjoying the prize, I hope. Ha ! ha ! ha !'

" There can be no doubt the skipper must have endured much agony from the treatment he had received, and been anxious to retaliate upon the pirates; consequently I felt little surprise at the savage joy he manifested on beholding the raging flames that were fast enveloping the brig in its fury.

" We could distinctly see the pirates making useless efforts to extinguish the flames, for so dazzling was the blaze from the combustible nature of the cargo, that the sea for a quarter of a mile around was like a sheet of crimson.

" ' They will get it presently, lad,' shouted the skipper in his excitement ; ' there is a ton of powder in kegs in the hold : they will have a second edition of the evening's amusement.'

" He had scarcely uttered the words before the brig was lifted, as it were, out of the water, and rent asunder, and driven in fragments high into the air. For a moment it appeared like the crater of a volcano—a wide blaze of bright light, millions of fiery atoms, driven in every direction, and in a few more seconds we were wrapped in the gloom of an intensely dark night; another minute and all was as still and quiet as if the peaceful ocean had never been witness to such a scene of desolation and death.

" ' There, my lad, the play is over; the reptiles have had their quietus. We may lie down till morning, for there will be no wind for the present, and I feel as if my feet didn't belong to my legs. I have half-a-dozen cutlass gashes in my body, and one of the swarthy villains made a cushion of my thighs to stick his knife in, because I kicked him while he was tying me. Curse them! I have had my revenge.'

" The skipper took a pull at the spirit jar, and after satisfying his thirst, handed it to me. I took a little, but drank copiously of the water. We wrapped ourselves in the large sail of the boat, and in spite of the skipper's wounds and my confusion of thoughts, we slept soundly and long.

" In the morning I was roused by the captain, who was so stiff with his wounds and lacerated ankles that he was almost unable to move.

" ' We must step the mast, my lad,' he said' 'before the breeze rises, for I can scarcely put my feet to the task of bearing my unlucky carcase ; we can do it best while it is calm.'

" With some difficulty we stepped the mast, and prepared the yard and sail for hoisting. The boat was nearly five-and-thirty feet in length and very broad, having been built for the purpose of landing a cargo, where no boats or conveniences could be procured, on the coast of the Black Sea.

" Immediately after sun-rise a stiff breeze from the eastward arose, and we hoisted our canvas; the skipper told me to steer dead before the wind, as the coast of Spain was ahead, and that before night we should see it, as it could not be more than a hundred miles from us.

" The captain evidently suffered severely, but having washed his wounds with the spirits, which I thought would inflame them, but which he swore would cure them, he lay down along the stern sheets and relieved me at times steering. We saw several vessels during the day, but very distant from us. The boat sailed remarkably well, and before the sun went down, the coast of Spain was distinctly visible.

" The skipper said he should make the coast somewhere between Malaga and Cape de Galle. Towards sun-down we observed a craft standing out from the land, close hauled, which my companion said would no doubt turn out to be one of the Spanish *guarda costas*, and in another hour we distinctly made her out. She was a large vessel, and appeared to go very rapidly through the water.

" 'That fellow will overhaul us,' said the captain ; ' it is a very unusual thing at this hour to see a boat like ours standing in for the land, unless it is a contrabandist's, and from the open sea.'

" He was right ; in less than half-an-hour the Spaniard was close to us, and after firing a musket, hove to. The skipper took the tiller and ran our boat alongside the Spanish guard-boat.

" There was a numerous crew aboard, and they looked over the side at us with considerable surprise. Their chief officer came to examine us, and listened to the skipper's account of our mishap with astonishment and considerable exultation. He spoke in *lingua franca*, which I understood well, and I heard him say to the skipper, 'you have rid the coast of one of the most desperate of the Salee rovers, commanded by one of the most ferocious cut-throats that ever infested those seas.' He insisted upon the skipper going aboard his craft, and when told I was the supercargo, very politely invited me also. He was bound for Carthagena. We were eastward of the Cape de Galle, and it would, therefore, be all the same to us to be landed at Carthagena or Malaga. We accordingly went on board; our boat was taken in tow, and we descended to the cabin.

" It was decidedly a change for the better. There was not the slightest chance of the skipper's story being contradicted, of course he gave himself out as the captain of the brig; the owner's name was plainly to be seen on the stern. The only difference he made was, that the brig was bound for Gibraltar instead of the Black Sea.

" We were hospitably treated by the worthy captain of the *guarda costa*, and the wind shifting two points more to the southward, we ran into the fine harbour of Carthagena the following evening.

" The captain landed us, leaving us our boat, which the skipper said he intended selling to pay our expenses back to Genoa, and sailed the following day for Barcelona with stores.

" We took up our abode at a first-rate *locanda*; our story ran like wildfire through the city, and everybody, high and low, crowded the inn to see the two Italians who had destroyed the xebecque of the notorious Mustafa Re.

" The landlord made his profit of us, and
we lived like princes without a stiver in our
pockets. The skipper sent for a surgeon, for
his legs were awfully inflamed, and while he
was getting well, I amused myself in walking
about the town, accepted numerous invitations,
and enjoyed myself, till an opportunity should
occur of getting to Genoa, and the skipper to
Palermo. He said he had no fear of being
found out, for he intended, the moment he
could collect what little property he had in
Palermo, to sail to the West Indies, and
pressed me to accompany him; but I felt no
inclination to follow his desperate fortunes any
longer than necessity compelled.

" Our boat was sold for a good sum, and
we were congratulating ourselves on our
good fortune, one morning at breakfast, when
four officers of justice entered the room, and
politely bowing and producing a paper,
after looking at it for a moment, one of the
officers said, speaking to the skipper :

"'Your name, captain, 'tis, I believe, Benedetto Lotero?'

"'Yes, said the skipper, 'so I call myself. Curse 'em, what's in the wind now,' he added, looking at me, and speaking in Italian.

"'And yours,' said the officer, turning to me, 'Julio Vachero?'

"'That's the name I was always known by' I replied.

"'Very good,' said the Spaniard, looking again at the paper in his hand. 'You were captain of the brig "Ida," owner, the Signor Matteo Gavotti?' addressing Malatesta.

"'Curse it, man,' interrupted the worthy Luigi, 'what the devil are you driving at? Can't you work your course dead on end, and not be tacking and staying like a lubberly Dutch dogger? What are you up to?'

"'Why only this, captain; that the vessel was not bound for Gibraltar, but for the Black Sea; and both of you are accused of

L 5

running away with the brig, after having murdered the owner's daughters on the coast of Corsica.   The short and long of the matter is, you are both accused of piracy on the high seas.'

" 'Very good,' replied Luigi Malatesta, quite coolly, and drinking off his hot cup of coffee, 'and pray officer, what is the name of our accuser?'

" 'One Captain Barracco, commanding the bark "Doria." He came into port last night from Genoa.'

"All this conversation I heard without feeling in the slightest degree alarmed. I felt sorry for the skipper, in spite of his rough manner,s his piratical seizure of the brig, and his making me his companion in spite of myself. I knew I could easily clear myself from the charge against me; indeed I was surprised at being included in the impeachment, as I was well known to Captain Barracco, whose name I remembered at once, having often met him in Genoa.

" While these thoughts were passing through my mind, the Spanish officer requested us to get ready to follow him to the judge appointed to hear our case, and in whose court we should find our accuser, Captain Barracco. We were soon ready.

On leaving the *locanda* we were surrounded by a rascally rabble of the lower orders, who saluted us by cursing us as a couple of rascally pirates, and after a time pelting us with mud; but the officers interfering, we reached the court house without further molestation. We found several of the principal inhabitants assembled from curiosity, and Captain Barracco awaiting our arrival.

"The magistrate and his clerk having taken their seats, the Genoese captain opened the case by stating that, when in Genoa, he had heard from the Signor Gavotti's son of the manner in which his father had lost his brig; his two sisters, and the lady to whose care they had been entrusted, having returned from Corsica. They informed their father that the skipper, Benedetto Lotero, and the supercargo, Julio Vachero, had planned the piracy of the vessel.

"'Avast there, captain,' roared Luigi Malatesta; 'that's a cursed lie; the lad there—'

"'Silence that man,' shouted the judge to the officers of the court, in a loud, angry tone. 'Signor Capitano, be so good as to continue.'

"'A cursed set of lying lubbers,' grumbled my worthy skipper, between his teeth.

"'That is all, your worship," said Captain Barracco.' 'I am ready to take oath that what I have stated is fact, and am willing to swear that man before me,' pointing to the skipper, 'is Captain Benedetto Lotero, and that youth, Julio Vachero.'

"'Ha! ha! ha!' laughed the skipper, 'don't perjure yourself, my worthy. If you swear that, you'll swear a lie, my hearty.'

" Captain Barracco looked daggers at the skipper, who laughed in his face.

" ' This morning early,' continued the Genoese Captain, ' I saw the long boat of the brig " Ida," hauled upon the jetty. I read the name and the owner's name as well. I was excessively astonished, and upon making enquiries, the accounts I heard induced me to lay my present charge before you ; and now that I have seen the prisoners, I feel satisfied my charge is correct.'

" Captain Barracco was then sworn, and repeated his charge.

" 'What have you to say to this charge of pirating the brig " Ida," from her owner, the Signor Matteo Gavotti ?' demanded the judge of Luigi Malatesta.

" 'Just what I told you before; that fellow,' pointing to Captain Barracco, ' has perjured himself. In the first place, my name is not Benedetto Lotero. I shall say nothing more, except that this lad had no more to do with

the charge made against him than you had.
That's all I have to say to you, so make the
most of it.'

"The Judge was amazingly angry, conversed in a low tone, first with a person near
him, and who I judged was a lawyer, and
then with his clerk.   After a minute he
turned towards us, saying : —

" 'I shall commit you as pirates. You will
be detained here, in prison, till an opportunity
occurs of sending you to Genoa, where you
will be tried by the laws of the Republic.
Officers, take them to the bagnio, and keep
them separate.'

"These orders were strictly obeyed.   You
may conceive, Count, my dismay, and indeed rage, on finding myself a prisoner,
in one of the most frightful sinks of ini-
quity the imagination can fancy. I mean
the bagnio or prison of the galley slaves, for
there it was we were confined, in dismal, dirty
cells, and badly fed.   The only air and exer-

cise we were allowed was in a large court, amid a whole gang of the lowest description of ruffians.

"I will not tire you with an account of all I suffered a period of nearly nine months, during which time I was never allowed to go out at the same hour as Luigi Malatesta. We were treated in every respect like condemned convicts, except not being branded or clothed in the galley attire; but our food and general treatment were the same. One morning the jailer entered my cell, with an assistant, and placed on my wrists a pair of handcuffs, telling me to follow him. I did so. In an outer chamber I saw the skipper, also handcuffed. He held out his hand to me, and shook mine heartily, saying :—

"'Don't be down-hearted, my lad. Cheer up, we are going at last to be sent out of this hell-upon-earth—curse 'em! There's a Sardinian brig-of-war outside; we shall be taken to Genoa. Never fear, I will clear you anyhow.'

" The skipper was right; we were taken
on board the "Ajax," a fine gun brig, bound to
Genoa, which city we reached in six days,
were landed, and again placed in separate
cells, in the city prison.   Even this was a relief; we were free from the horrid blasphemy
of the galley slaves, and the disgusting filth
of the Bagnio of Carthagena.'

" I felt in better spirits, expecting every
hour a visit from my poor mother, as well as
getting released, by the order of Signor
Gavotti, who must have been convinced by
his daughters, long ago, that I was quite
innocent of pirating away his brig ' Ida.'
Several days passed, and no human being
except the jailor entered my cell; and all
the answer I could get from that brute was,
' if I did not hold my jaw he would put me
in irons.'

" A fortnight passed after our arrival
before our trial came on.   I was almost in
despair.   Where was my mother?   Could

she be dead! I shuddered as the thought swept through my mind. Was it possible that the daughters of the Signor Gavotti could know of my cruel imprisonment and not make some effort to assist me, whom they knew to be innocent?

" In the court, which was crowded, I saw the faces of many persons I knew, but not one returned the look of recognition I cast upon them. Anxiously I gazed from the dock into the crowded court, and up to the galleries, but nowhere could I see my mother. There were several prisoners to be tried, but our case came on first.

" I do not intend wearying you with the details of that detestable day, which threw a shadow over the whole of my future existence. I discovered, during the progress of the trial, that Signor Matteo Gavotti was dead, that his son inherited his property, and that he it was who prosecuted us. My mother I learned was no longer in Genoa ;

when or why she left the city, no one took the trouble to inform me. When I enquired for the two daughters of the Signor Gavotti, to prove my innocence, I was told that the eldest was married, and that the two youngest were with her in Florence. The oath of Luigi Malatesta that I was innocent was perfectly unheeded.

"It was proved by Captain Barracco, who found us at Carthagena, that I was living in perfect amity and fellowship with Luigi Malatesta at a first rate *locando* in that city : that the sale of the boat and our living on the money obtained for it, proved our partnership in the crime of piracy. Our judge was well known as the severest and sternest of all the Republic's magistrates. To my intense rage and vexation we were condemned. My blood runs cold even now, Count, when I recall to memory the events of that day. Luigi Malatesta was condemned to be branded and sent to the galleys for life.

CHAPTER XIV.

"In consideration of my youth I was sentenced to the galleys for seven years, and to be branded on the right shoulder. I knew not what I said or did when I heard this unjust sentence passed upon me. I only remember that the judge said sternly, 'take care, young man, or perhaps the seven years may be changed to double that number.'

"I was conveyed back to prison. The next day I was to be branded and sent to Lavera. In the evening of that day, two jailors, with assistants and a smith, conducting another prisoner, entered my cell. They carried chains in their hands, and immediately the smith and assistants commenced the operation of chaining me to the convict they brought into my cell. Resistance was out of the question, though I was bursting with rage, and tortured with anxiety.

" My fellow convict, a tall, powerful man, with by no means an unprepossessing countenance, talked, laughed, and joked with the turnkey, as if the operation performing was the pleasantest in the world. First a massive ring of iron was rivetted round my left ankle; from this a heavy chain led to an iron belt round the waist of my fellow convict. A similar ring was rivetted on his ankle; which led to a belt round my waist. This was padlocked. Havi ng thus fastened us to each other, they left us to our supper, saying with a laugh—' To-morrow morning you will have your uniform, and the big G will be put on your shoulder.'

"I suppose I shuddered with disgust at the disgrace and ignominy about to be inflicted on me. The turnkey perceived it, and with a grin said:

"'Ah! you are thinking of the hot iron. It's a mere nothing—we do things nicely—only crumps up the flesh a little. We don't like, you see, to lose our children when once we get them; so we mark 'em.'

"As soon as we were left alone, I sat down on the stone bench in despair. My companion stood for a moment looking at me, for we were allowed a lamp that would burn for two hours, and then sitting beside me, ate with an exceedingly good appetite.

"'You are down in the mouth, comrade,' said the man; 'I was in the Court during your trial. I think you are innocent, in fact, I could swear you are.'

"I looked up in the man's face in some surprise, saying 'What makes you think so?'

"'I will tell you, comrade,' replied the man;

'but first let me save some of the oil of that
lamp; we shall want it presently, as you
will see.'

"We arose, for our movements, owing to
the infernal chain that linked us, made us de-
pendent on each other.   He poured out some
of the oil into the tin can we drank out of,
and then reseating ourselves, he said :

" ' I will tell you why I think you are innocent.   During your examination by the
judge, I overheard the conversation of two
men leaning on the rails of the dock against
which I was standing.   It's useless repeating
what they said, but I heard enough to satisfy
me that you owed your conviction to the enmity
of your prosecutor, the young Gavotti.   I believe the men were his own domestics, for they
spoke of his sisters, and how they had heard
them say you did all you could, when aboard
the brig you were accused of pirating, to
save and console them when you found the
skipper was a pirate.   It's very little conso-

lation, however,' added the man, ' to feel you are innocent. I would rather have done something to deserve my sentence.'

" ' I differ with you,' I replied ; ' but tell me what was your offence ?'

" ' Oh! not much,' carelessly replied my comrade. ' I am one of the famous brigands of the Bochetta. You have heard of us, I daresay.'

" ' Yes,' I replied; ' I have heard a great many tales of your daring combination, and how, for many years, you have defied the powers of the Republic to root you out of your mountain retreat.

" My companion laughed merrily, saying ' They will never be able to root us out. But listen to me, comrade; I have taken a fancy to you.'

" I looked at the man who was to be my companion for the next seven years—if we lived that time—not rightly comprehending his strange, careless manner, while I was almost maddened at the thought of the horrid degradation I was doomed to undergo on the morrow.

"He was a tall, muscular man, about three and thirty years of age, with a countenance dark and sunburnt, but a good-humoured expression—nothing of the ferocity of a brigand about him.

"'Well, comrade, it is getting time for us to act. Now, I'll give you your choice of what I expect you will call two evils. Will you join our band and take the oaths, or be branded as a felon, and pass seven years of your young life, chained as you now are, working like a slave and doomed to the lash of a brutal overseer?'

"I started from the bench, and stood looking at the man with astonishment.

"'Are you mad, or dreaming? Do you know where you are? Have you forgotten these baubles?' and I clanked the chains that were galling me almost to madness.

" ' Oh! they are mere trifles to what you will get after the branding. Never heed the baubles, as you call them. Answer my question : will you or will you not join our band ? If I procure your freedom, will you take the oaths?'

" ' Yes,' I exclaimed firmly, but considerably excited.

" ' Good.'

" ' Yes, give me freedom, and I will join any community that wars with the human race; ever since the hour I was so unjustly and cruelly condemned, my blood has been boiling within me. But you talk of improbabilities, if not impossibilities.'

" ' Not at all,' replied the brigand coolly. ' Do you see that window, with its four strong iron bars?'

" I looked up mechanically ; there was a window, certainly, strongly barred, through which the light faintly entered. It was about twelve feet from the floor of our cell. I

laughed in bitterness of soul, as I looked alternately at its security and our heavy fetters.

"'Attend to what I say,' said the convict ;
'in four hours, at the farthest, we must be
ready to get through that window.   Listen !
here comes our gaoler for the lamp.   I have
been waiting for that; after he closes the door
against us, we shall remain unvisited till the
morning.'

"The   bolts   were   shot back,   the door
unlocked, and the turnkey entered ; and, after
examining our manacles and seeing all right,
retired, taking away the lamp.   A strong ray
of moonlight entered our cell through the bars,
for there was no glass.

"'Ah !' said my comrade, 'we are much
obliged to bright Phœbus ; but we must make
the most of her kindness, for she will be down
by the time we are ready.   Now, let us to
work.   That window looks out upon the harbour, and underneath is the rampart that runs
all round the port; it's about fifty feet from

the wall. I know every inch of this building. First, however, let us get rid of these orna· ments,' and he laughed heartily.

" Taking off his shoes, to my great surprise, he took from between the soles five extraordinarily thin and minute saws, and two equally thin files and a knife-blade.

" ' You see, comrade, we carry our tools with us. I suppose you never used tools of this description, so you must count on lacerating your fingers a little ; but that's not as bad as branding,' and he gave me a dig on the shoulder; ' so let us get to work.'

" We went close under the light, that I might observe the way he used the saws, which he informed me were made from the same steel as the mainsprings of watches.

" The man went to work with such energy and skill, that in less than an hour he had actually freed his leg from the chain, but leaving the ring round his ankle, for that it would be impossible to remove.

" I worked vigorously, so hard, indeed, that the perspiration rolled from my head and face in drops as large as peas. He, however, was obliged to help me, for not being accustomed to the fine tools, I did not make the progress he did. In little more than another half-hour, my leg was freed. In less time we divided the link confining the chains to the waist. I asked no questions, but obeyed all my comrade's instructions.

" Our next task was to cut up the whole of our bedding and covering into strips, and finally twisting it into a strong rope of above sixty feet. After accomplishing this, and trying the strength of our rope, yard by yard, we raised the frame of the oak bedstead against the wall and commenced operations upon the iron bars, two of which tried all our strength alternately for two hours, my hands bleeding a good deal ; even my comrade's hands suffered in this operation, and I unfortunately broke two of the saws. The files, however, did us good service.

" By this time the moon had set, and the night, in less than an hour, became gloomy and overcast. We could hear the bell of the Annunciat a toll the fourth hour of the morning as we fastened our rope to the two remaining bars. I must confess my heart beat strangely, while my companion was as cool and as unconcerned as if it were for pastime we were working. The oil of the lamp proved of essential service; in fact, I doubt if we could have accomplished cutting through the bars without it. The rope was knotted at intervals, so that our descent might be less hazardous. As my comrade prepared to descend, he whispered—

" ' Not one word now, for on each side of us are two sentinels, about a hundred yards distant. They belong to the garrison, not the prison. Utter no sound, even should you suffer.'

" The next instant he passed his body through the opening, and slid down the rope. I lost sight of him in the gloom and fog that rose from the water of the harbour, over the rampart. I waited a minute, and then thrusting myself out of the window, with little difficulty, reached the rampart. The rope had proved quite long enough.

" The fog was very dense, and that, added to the darkness of the night, rendered it impossible to see more than a couple of yards ahead. My companion placed his hand upon my arm, whispering in my ear—

" ' Most likely the sentinel is in his box; steal along with your hands on the wall; when we reach his box, our united strength will enable us to pitch it over on its face ; that will settle its lazy inmate for a time. Fifty yards farther will take us to the steps leading down into the street. Keep close to me then, and in less than half-an-hour we shall be as safe as if on the summit of the Bochetta.'

" My comrade was right; the sentinel was in his box, quietly humming a tune. Silently, we placed our shoulders against it, and at the same instant putting forth our united strength, heaved it over on its face. It went upon the ramparts with a loud crash, and a smothered exclamation of pain and terror from the astonished soldier.

" Springing over the box, we hurried on, gained the steps, and in another minute were in the long, dismal street—chiefly occupied by braziers and tin-workers—that runs along the harbour wall from the Porto del Mare, nearly to the arsenal. Along this my companion led the way, and turning down a narrow lane, continued for nearly half-an-hour, twisting and turning through a part of the city I knew no more of than I do of New York. Suddenly he paused, in a very narrow street, on each side of which the houses were exceedingly lofty, and entering beneath an archway, he stopped at a door, and I believed pulled some kind of bell or signal, for in less than five minutes the door swung open.

"'Hold my arm,' said my guide.

"I did so; and then I heard the door close, seemingly of itself. The darkness was impenetrable; but my conductor walked steadily along the passage till we came to a flight of stone-stairs, up which we went, still in darkness, till we stopped at a second door. Against this he gave five peculiar knocks, and presently a small panel opened, and a voice issued from it, there was no light, saying—

"' Five times five.'

"'Double it,' said my companion, 'and it will make fifty.'

" Immediately the door fell back, and we passed in. Still I saw no one; we evidently walked along a corridor for about twenty yards, and then my companion opened a door; and for the first time light fell upon surrounding objects.

"'Follow me,' said my comrade; 'but utter not a word till I address you.'

" We passed through the door and

entered a very large and lofty saloon. I was
startled at what I saw on entering the room.
I first of all perceived a large fire facing me,
and in the middle of the room stood a massive
and rather large table, on which were
scattered every variety of edibles of all kinds,
flasks and jars of wine, goblets and glasses—
some upset and some broken, and a quantity
of wine flowing from the table to the floor.
Along one side of this chamber were ranged
about a dozen broad benches, on one of which
a male figure was sleeping, covered only with
a mantle—a thin mattress formed his bed;
others were sleeping in different parts of the
room. Only one of the sleepers raised his
head as we entered ; he looked, stupidly at
first, at my comrade, but getting more awake,
or quickly recognising him, he started to his
feet with a loud oath, saying in a rough,
though joyful tone : —

" ' By the bones of St. Anthony! this is a
surprise. Your hand, Captain. But who the

devil is the strange bird you have brought
with you ?'

" 'All in good time, Jerome.   Hallo! they
are all awake now.'

"And true enough, in less than two
minutes twelve rough and certainly very
suspicious-looking individuals had roused
from their sleep and surrounded my comrade,
each shaking him heartily by the hand.

" He whispered something in the ear of
each, evidently concerning me, for they all
offered me their hand, shaking mine heartily,
wishing me to join them in a glass to our
healths, and congratulating me on my escape
from the branding iron.   This being done, my
comrade took me by the arm, led me to the
further end of the room, and opening a door,
shewed me another chamber very similar to
the one we were in, though not so large.   In
it were several of the same kind of beds along
the walls ; giving me a lamp, he said :

" There, get two or three hours' rest ; it is

contrary to the rules for a new member to stay with the brotherhood till he has taken the oaths. In the morning, or rather in a few hours, there will be a smith here to relieve us from these elegant jewels. Farewell for the present.'

" He left me to my own reflections, which were not so painful as might have been anticipated, for youth and fatigue, and joy at escaping the ignominy of the branding iron of the galley slave, banished all other thoughts, and in a few minutes 1 was sound asleep— on certainly a very hard bed, without covering of any sort.

" It is not in my power, Count, to tell you the nature of the oaths I took the next day, before the men who are the city comrades of the mountain band. Our manacles were taken, by a smith, from our ankles. I suffered greatly, for the iron being riveted too tightly, had galled my leg sadly.

" My comrade of the prison was no less a

person than the Captain of the band I now command.

" ' I can tell you something,' said one of the men who sat next me at breakfast that morning, ' that will give you some clue to the enmity with which the younger Gavotti prosecuted you.' I had related my story to the man. ' You had a mother and sister, had you not ?'

" ' Yes,' I replied, looking anxiously at the speaker.

" ' Well, then,' continued the man, ' the younger Gavotti wanted to have your sister on his own terms.'

" ' What !' I exclaimed, the blood rushing to my face and temples, ' how do you know that? I am not aware they had ever met.'

" Ah ! but I know better,' said the man, with a knowing grin ; ' you see we occasionally do trifling jobs for the young nobility and gentry here in the city. In fact, anything, if the purse offered is well filled. Well, your sister did not like the offer of the youngster, but he was determined to have her. Our city band services are always to be had by following certain rules, and this young Gavotti got an introduction to our Captain. I don't mean your Capitano ; we have a city Captain of our own; and offered a good round sum to him to carry off the girl and take her to his father's country house at Nervi, which at the time was uninhabited.'

"I did not speak, but listened with the greatest anxiety, my blood boiling with rage. The man continued:

" 'You are now one of us, therefore I may tell you all I know. Jerome and I were appointed to manage the girl—excuse me, comrade—your worthy little sister, I mean, and a pretty and virtuous girl she was—'

" ' Was !' I interrupted, in a hoarse voice. ' By heaven ! if the villain has dared to destroy—'

" 'At the moment I was speaking, the door of the apartment was violently thrown open, and two or three of the band rushed into the room ; they were in a great state of excitement.'

" ' What's the matter ?' asked the man I had been talking to.

" ' The city is in a state of violent tumult. Every quarter has poured forth its inhabitants — a bloody warfare is this moment raging in the streets against the Austrian garrison.'

" This intelligence caused great commotion amongst the community. They whispered together for several moments, and then dispersed.

" 'Come with me,' said my companion of the breakfast table, whose name in the band was Vincentio Mola. ' We may show ourselves anywhere in the city we please. The mob have attacked and broken open the prisons, and turned out the inmates, provided them with arms, and in fact every soul of the lower order of the people is roused into mad rage against their cursed oppressors, the Austrians.

Many of the mansions of the nobility and wealthy merchants will be pillaged during the outbreak, for there are hundreds always ready for that kind of work during popular commotions.'

" All this time my thoughts were dwelling upon my unfortunate sister and her brutal oppressor—the younger Gavotti.   I placed a pair of pistols, Mola gave me, in my pockets, and each taking a cutlass from the stores, we sallied forth, completely undisguised, into the streets.

" I will explain in a few words, the cause of this last and glorious effort of the people of Genoa to put down their tyrannous conquerors. Some short time before the Austrian general, Botto Adorno, had been admitted into the city, at the head of fifteen thousand men. No sooner was he in possession than he took the most insulting and oppressive advantage of the miserable cowardice of the Senate.   His monstrous rapacity and the insolence of his troops exceeded all human forbearance.

" In less than three months he had extorted contributions to the amount of twenty-four millions of florins ; his troops were suffered to commit the most brutal excesses among the citizens and peasantry. Many of the nobles were exiled, the Great National Bank of St. George was totally drained of its treasures, and failed; the church plate and the property of private individuals were ruthlessly seized. In fact, they left the miserable people nothing but life to lose.

" At this period of furious rage against their oppressors, when the goaded and suffer-ing people still retained sufficient courage—and merited a better government than their degenerate oligarchy—the main Austrian army passed out into Provence.   Botta Adorno despatched a great part of his artillery from the arsenal to assist at the siege of Antibes.

" On the very morning of my escape from prison, an accident gave rise to the insurrection ;   the long-smothered hatred of the people burst forth. In removing a heavy mortar, its carriage broke down; the Austrian officer in command insolently and brutally struck a Genoese who was passing, and who had indignantly refused to put his shoulder to the carriage. The Genoese boldly resented this petty tyrant, and wounded him, and the crowd assembled attacked the Austrian party with a shower of stones. Like magic, the whole body of the lower orders flew to arms.

" The Genoese garrison, confounded by the sudden revolt, attacked on all sides, entangled in the narrow streets, and crushed and wounded by every kind of missile thrown from the windows and house tops, were over powered and defeated in detail.

" Such was the state of affairs as, following my companion, I found myself in the crowded and tumultuous streets of the city. All I shall say of the insurrection is, that in four-

and twenty hours the Austrians were driven in disgrace from the city.

"I will relate one incident that occurred to myself during the tumult of that memorable day. Following a formidable band of the people, who were going to fortify a house that stood in a most favourable position for defence, I perceived a rabble breaking into a mansion I recognized, at a glance, to be the residence of the late Matteo Gavotti. 'Those are plunderers,' said I to Vincentio Mola, who was close beside me, 'and that house is Gavotti's. By heaven! I will see if I cannot have a word with the villain who ruined my family and has disgraced me for ever.' And as soon as the front door was broken down I crushed through the mob, and was one of the first who entered the house and rushed up the great staircase leading from the hall. On the first landing-place stood several domestics armed, and at their head I at once recognized Ludovico Gavotti.

" In my eagerness I became foremost of
the rabble ; Gavotti knew me immediately,
and with a bitter curse he leveled a pistol at
my head. I felt the ball enter my left
shoulder, but it seemed only the sharp point
of a cold instrument entering my flesh, and I
rushed at the youth like a maniac. The
mob shouted and cursed frightfully, and the
servants fled in terror. Before Gavotti could
discharge a second pistol I caught him by
the throat, and being by far the stronger
man, I dragged him into the adjoining apartment, he struggling violently. The room
was nearly empty, for, anticipating something
might happen during the insurrection, the servants had removed the valuables to a place of
safety. The mob dispersed over the house,
seeking plunder. I remained alone with my
victim, who was a coward at heart; I held
my cutlass to his throat, and in a low but
bitter voice I asked him where was his
victim, my sister Julia. My blood boiled at

the thoughts of all the wrong I and my family
had suffered at his hands, and I cursed him;
swearing that hour should be his last if he
did not tell the truth.

"'Your sister was no victim of
mine,' said Gavotti, in a hoarse and tremb-
ling voice ; 'you will not murder me for nothing ?'

"'Nothing, villain,' I repeated. 'Are you
speaking the truth? Where are my mother
and sister? Answer me truly, or by the
heaven above you shall die.'

"'I tell you I never injured your sister,
further than having her and her mother
carried to my country house at Nervi. I
solemnly swear that ere I could see her there,
she and her mother, with the woman who had
the care of them, escaped, and got across the
mountains; but to what place I know not.
I loved her from the first moment I saw her.
I swore she should be mine, on my own
terms; but she escaped me.'

" ' Admitting this to be true, what did I do to incur the bitter hatred with which you persecuted me, knowing in your heart I was guiltless of any act detrimental to your father's interest ?'

" ' First, I hated you because your sister threatened me with chastisement at your hands; and I doubly hated you because—' and he paused.

" ' Because what ? ' I demanded.

" ' Because my sister Laurina loved you, and I swore you should never have her for a wife.'

" ' Great heaven ! ' I exclaimed, ' and for such paltry causes have you, you miserable wretch, condemned me body and soul;' and with a feeling of intense abhorrence I cast him from me, and turned to quit the room, when the door opened, and Vincentio Mola entered, saying :

" ' Be quick, I have kept good watch for you. Let us away, a body of the people are coming to turn this house into a fortress. The plunderers have decamped, let us be off. In an hour we must quit the city, and get to our mountain retreat.'

" The story of my life is nearly finished. Before night of the following day, I reached this cave with my Captain, Vincentio Mola; and for three years I followed him in all his undertakings. He was neither bloodthirsty nor rapacious—twice I saved his life ; and when, a year after, he was slain by a pistol shot from a *gens d'arme*, he insisted on the band selecting me as their captain.

" This caused a division of our force ; the fiercest and most ferocious followed Marco Remini, and took up their residence in the mountain fastnesses near Aqui.

" I tried every means in my power to discover the retreat of my mother and sister, but in vain. I could never gain the slightest clue to their whereabouts, and know not whether they are still in existence. I have laboured hard to render my men less ferocious in their contests with the *gens d'armes* ; it used to be the plan to lie in ambush behind rocks, where they could not be pursued, except on foot, and shoot down all the unfortunate *gens d'armes* on their passage across the Bochetta. Now they are never attacked unless they persist in defending the travellers they are bound to escort ; and this rarely happens, for we are so well apprised by our spies, and others in our pay, of the number and condition of those we intend to waylay, that we generally adopt the plan we pursued when we attacked the Countess di Sera and entrap them without bloodshed.

" I have nothing more to say, Count, only to express my deep regret in allowing my passions to overpower my reason. I was condemned to a frightful fate, while perfectly innocent, and I grasped, perhaps naturally, at anything that offered a prospect of escape.

Had I waited in prison till morning, the insurrection of the people would have given me freedom ; the skipper, Luigi Malatesta, was released and escaped from Genoa, while I, despairing, and having no trust in a good Providence, rashly bound myself for life to become a robber.

" One consolation I have is that I have never stained my hands with blood in any of our encounters, nor ever fired at traveller or soldier since I joined the band. I have, however, made myself so useful to them in many ways that they have invariably refused to cancel my oaths, and unless they commit some outrage upon my liberty, I cannot in conscience resign my command."

The Count de Briesbach heard the brigand to the end, with but few remarks. He pitied him, for he said that he had been grievously wronged ; though he could not help feeling that the great fault in the man's career had been his being so easily persuaded into adopting a life of infamy to escape the degradation of being branded as a galley slave.

" You are thinking, Count," said the robber, " that had you been placed in the same situation you would have borne the degradation, which was unjustly to be inflicted, in preference to selecting a life of infamy, the end of which must be either death or the very fate from which I fled. Death shall rid me from the latter, sooner—"

" There again," interrupted the Count, " your passion and fear of worldly scorn and opprobium, are rendering you totally forgetful of another world beside the one we live in. No! cast off the chain that binds you. I do not mean to advise you to betray your companions—that would be infamous; but if they refuse to let you depart, go without their leave to some distant land. You are young, stout of heart, and may yet regain the esteem of your fellow men. I cannot consider oaths binding made to men leading a life of infamy—men, whose occupation and pursuits involve the breaking of every tie, human and divine. However, I will say no more for the present; it is late, and I trust to-morrow will bring some intelligence that will enable you to release the unfortunate young lady from her cruel and painful position."

"I sincerely hope so," said the Captain; "but there is disunion in our band, and much discontent. I am looked upon with suspicion; my refusal to demand ransom for you has caused much grumbling."

"In sooth," replied the Count, smiling, "they need not quarrel with you for that; as far as my ransom is concerned, they may demand what sum they please; but getting it from a poor soldier of fortune—that is quite out of the question."

"Well, Count, I will wish you good night, and trust that this affair will turn out better than I anticipate. I will think over what you said just now; but to my mind, an oath is an oath—no matter how or to whom given."

So saying, the brigand Captain left the Count to his repose.

CHAPTER XV.

On the eastern coast of Corsica, on the side of a hill, stands the town of Bastia. At the period of our tale it was considered the capital of the island by the Genoese, who still held it in their hands. The whole interior of the island was in a state of open revolt. Many of the towns along the west coast had been attacked, the soldiers of the Republic being either driven out or massacred, and the people restored to liberty and their ancient laws. Unassisted, the Genoese found it impossible to resist the determined attacks of the islanders; the war was, therefore, carried on, on both sides, with unrelenting animosity and cruelty.

A large number of the Genoese nobility and gentry inhabited the town of Bastia, who were terribly alarmed at the state of things throughout the island. One of these noblemen, Phillippo Carignano, was at this period governor of Corsica. He was of a high, but impoverished family, and had accepted the dangerous post at a time when there appeared every probability that the power of Genoa, over this ill-treated island, was drawing to its close.

The Marchese de Carignano was a widower and advanced in life; his family consisted of a son and daughter. It was to the interest of the nobles to promote dissensions, which they turned to good account, by either confiscating the estates of the islanders, or condemning them to pay enormous fines, which went chiefly into the governor's or commissary-general's private coffers. It was also a common practice with the governor to condemn numbers to the galleys in order that they might purchase their freedom at a high price.

The Marchese de Carignano, not content with the plunder he had amassed, appointed his son commissary of Ajaccio, a circumstance fraught with misery to the Corsicans, for bad and corrupt as was the sire, the son was ten times worse. Francisco Count de Carignano was in his twenty-eighth year, and in Genoa was known as one of the most dissolute and most dissipated of the young nobility. He was tall and handsome, with very insinuating manners, but with a countenance strongly indicative of his character. He had the reputation of being brave and skilful in the use of the sword and pistol, and had more than once convinced the Corsicans that besides being a cruel, extortionate commissary he was no mean soldier.

After this brief sketch we must request our reader to accompany us into a large and well-furnished chamber, in the Castle of Bastia,

the residence of the commissary-general.   In
this chamber sat the Marchese de Carignano,
the table before him covered with papers and
letters.   Opposite to him was his secretary,
busily engaged writing what the governor
dictated.

In a deep recess of one of the large windows, which commanded an extensive view
of the harbour and the Mediterranean, sat
the Marchese's daughter, the Lady Bianca,
occupied in writing.   She was twenty years
of age, tall, well-formed, with dark eyes and
hair, handsome features, a clear and fine complexion, and richly habited.   The Marchese
continued dictating to his secretary letters to
the senate, stating the necessity that existed
for an immediate reinforcement of troops and
stores.   He was interrupted by the entrance
of a domestic, announcing the Count de
Matrà.   The Marchese instantly arose and
advanced a step or two to meet the Corsican,
as he was entering the room.

The two noblemen, after a very cordial greeting, advanced to where the lady Bianca was seated; and after a few enquiries and saluting the lady, who cordially returned his greeting, the Count de Matrà retired with the Marchese into the deep recess of another window, where they seated themselves.

There was a striking dissimilarity in the persons and dress of the two noblemen. The Marchese de Carignano was tall, somewhat thin, but very stately; the Count de Matrà was about the middle height, robust, and muscular, and some ten years younger than the Governor. His manner was abrupt and rather harsh. In his dress he adhered to the costume of the Corsicans, who were always extremely simple in their attire.

The Count de Matrà had great wealth and greater influence, and his siding with the Genoese was, in a great measure, the cause of the prolonged and bloody struggle that kept the island in a state of perpetual warfare for years; for had his influence, connection, and numerous vassals joined the patriots, the struggle would scarcely have lasted a year.

"Well, Count," said the Marchese, "I trust you have received more certain intelligence of your beloved daughter. It is a most distressing case; and when I return to Genoa, I will lay before the Senate a representation of the frightful evils caused by those brigands of the Bochetta, and urge some vigorous measure for putting down the marauders."

"That you can do," replied the Count; "but as far as I am concerned, I am happy to tell you that Vannina has escaped from the villanous bandits."

"Ha!" exclaimed the Governor, in a highly pleased tone; "this is, in truth, joyful and unexpected news. Where did you hear it? How on earth did the dear girl contrive to get free? I am quite astonished! Only three days ago you wrote to the Count de Rivalora to pay whatever sum was demanded for her ransom."

"I did; but Vannina was in Genoa before

that letter reached its destination," and the Count rubbed his large, bony hands with every appearance of satisfaction. "She has, thanks to the Virgin Mary, escaped without my paying those greedy rascals a single carlini."

" Excuse me, Count ; I must tell Bianca this good news. Three days ago she had a letter from her friend, the Countess di Sera, giving a long account of this sad affair. I have not heard the particulars, having been so much occupied with dictating letters to my secretary, who sails for Genoa with them to-morrow."

" The very reason, Marchese, I hurried over from Fiorenza. You mentioned your intention of sending your secretary, and that he would return immediately. I will despatch Vannina's nurse over, and he can take charge of them b ack."

" I was going to propose that my son should proceed to Genoa and escort back his betrothed ; I think your plan is better."

"Bianca, my dear girl, come here," exclaimed the Marchese.

Bianca joined the two noblemen.

"You will be surprised to learn that your friend, Vannina, about whom you have been so uneasy, is quite safe and well, and now under the protection of the Countess di Sera."

"What!" exclaimed the Lady Bianca, "has some one paid the immense sum the brigands demanded for her rescue; your letter, Count, could not have reached them."

"Rivalora's letter," replied the Count, smiling, "is not very explanatory. He merely says that through the agency and gallantry of a cavalier, named the Count de Briesbach, who was captured at the same time, Vannina was—"

"Count de Briesbach," said the governor, thoughtfully, "a young man?"

"I can't say,' replied de Matrà. "Rivalora said nothing about that; in truth he writes very strangely. I never heard him speak of this rebellion in the manner he does in his recent letter."

"I can enlighten you about this Count de Briesbach, father," replied the Lady Bianca. "The Countess di Sera's letters are full of his praises. She describes him as remarkably handsome, splendid figure, and of unquestionable gallantry. She says he has greatly distinguished himself during the late war in the Milanese, serving in the army of the King of Sardinia. She declares that his conversation is not alone pleasing, but positively brilliant."

The Marchese looked at his daughter whilst she was speaking, with a rather troubled expression, of countenance, while the Count de Matrà said, in a rough, but good humoured manner,—

"Why, Bianca, your friend the Countess has been describing an Adonis. The Genoese beauties will have to take care of their hearts."

"In sooth, Count," replied Bianca, with rather a sarcastic tone, "your fair daughter runs the greatest risk of losing her heart."

" Pooh ! " said the Count, " the hearts of girls at sixteen are very inflammable articles. Your amiable brother, Francisco, when she arrives, must charm away the image of this German Apollo."

" You think too lightly of maidens' hearts, Count," said Bianca, seriously. " You will find them stubborn things to bend, when once let loose, especially at Vannina's age."

" If your brother gets her hand," replied the Count de Matrà, rising, " he will, I fancy, soon succeed in securing her heart."

The Count and the governor left the room together, conversing earnestly upon the subject of the rebellion, as they termed it.

Bianca stood quietly gazing at the door through which her father and the Count had left the saloon ; and after a few minutes she walked over to the table, where sat the secretary. He raised his eyes—and dark, and brilliant, and wicked eyes they were—to the Lady Bianca, and then looked towards the door. He arose, and taking the unresisting

hand of the governor's daughter, led her towards the recess she had previously occupied.

"What marvellous intelligence is it, that
seems to have had such effect upon you all?
I caught a word or two, but could make
nothing out of it."

"Simply, Ludovico," replied Bianca, "that
my dear friend Vannina has escaped from the
brigands. But I feel certain that she is still
in bondage."

"I thought you said she was free?" said
the secretary.

"So I did; but, though she has bodily
escaped, her heart is captured, or I'm no
woman."

Bianca explained how the Count de
Matrà's daughter had escaped.

"My father and the Count have arranged,"
continued Bianca, "that you, Ludovico, are to
take charge of the wanderer home. Take care
of yourself; I know not how to trust you."
And the Governor's daughter looked keenly,

and, it must be confessed, somewhat doubtfully, into the young man's face.

"With your image so firmly impressed here," replied the youth, kissing the fair hand he held, and placing it on his breast, "what power could another's beauty have over me? my whole heart is yours, and yours only, dear Bianca. Surely you cannot doubt me, after all I undergo for you. Is it nothing to sit and write hour after hour, and listen day after day about these villanous islanders and their rebellious doings? and all for love of you, Bianca."

"Not quite that, Ludovico. Did not your own thoughtless extravagance and the necessity of doing something, after dissipating a noble fortune, induce you in the first instance to accept my father's offer of becoming his secretary, and the promise of the first vacant post of commissary in this island?"

"Which very enviable situation, my dear girl," added the handsome secretary, "he bestowed upon your worthy brother Francisco. So you ought to allow me some credit, besides a mercenary one, in this bargain with your father."

"Oh! yes, a little, Ludovico," said the Lady Bianca. "But let me warn you upon this subject of Vannina. I tell you, our future union depends in a great measure upon Francisco's marriage with this wealthy heiress. Owing to this insurrection, my father's governorship has turned out anything but lucrative. You know how embarrassed he was before he had this appointment. Your claims upon him are as far off being settled as ever. You have left yourself without resources; and I am portionless. To marry under such circumstances would be the height of folly."

"Upon my soul, Bianca, you weigh our love and future happiness in a very nice balance. When you knew that money was so essential to our union, in the name of for· tune why did you dissuade me from inter-

fering when your father gave the lucrative
post of commissary of Ajaccio to your brother.
He could not have refused to bestow it on me
if I had demanded it."

"The reason is very simple, Ludovico,"
said the governor's daughter calmly. "You
are no soldier, and Ajaccio, at the time of
Francisco's nomination, required a bold and
fearless leader, and one accustomed to warfare."

"Humph!" muttered the secretary, a
slight colour suffusing his face for a moment;
"and so, Bianca, you considered your lover
quite unfit to become a soldier. Perhaps," he
continued with some asperity, "you think
him a coward also ?"

" This is trifling, Ludovico. Did I think
so, there could be little love between us.
Now hear my other reason. On your return
from Genoa with the fair Vannina, my father
has promised me that he will get you appointed to the far better post of Commissary
of Calvi, one of the best and wealthiest towns
on the island; and which is surrounded by

the lands and domains of the Count de Matrà, who, you know, with all his numerous vassals sides with us."

" You are the dearest girl in the world, Bianca," said the secretary, kissing, not the hand, but the lips of the fair Genoese, " and I the most ungrateful of men. But is this fortunate intelligence certain? By Jove! just let me be Commissary of Calvi for two years, and I will ask no further favor of Dame Fortune than this fair hand."

" It is quite true. It was this very morning that my father told me he had got the post for you, but did not wish to tell you till after your return from Genoa. Another thing I was anxious to impart. The Count de Matrà wishes for a youthful companion for Vannina. She will be betrothed immediately after her arrival here; but the marriage will not take place till she has attained the age of eighteen, otherwise she would lose the fief of Monza, left her by her uncle, who made a most singular will. Could you not bring your sister Laurina back with you ?—she would, I am sure, be very happy with Vannina, and help to keep her, by her good spirits, from moping and thinking, and fancying herself in love with this handsome Count de Briesbach. I fear we shall have much trouble about this Count, judging from the letters of the Countess di Sera. You will see him, no doubt, at the Palace di Sera, and be able to form some judgment as to the state of affairs."

"As to the girl's being in love," said the secretary, in a careless tone, " it will signify very little. I have seen and heard a good deal of the stern and determined character of the Count de Matrà, and when he says his daughter shall marry Francisco Carignano, by Jove! she must marry him or go into a convent. Laurina will be glad to accompany Vannina, and quit the dull mansion of her present protectress. I will send for her im-

mediately on my arrival at Genoa, and introduce her to the heiress."

The daughter of the Governor of Corsica
and her lover, Ludovico Gavotti (for our
readers will have discovered who the handsome
secretary was), remained for nearly half-an-
hour in earnest conversation ere they separated; the former to make arrangements
for his departure for Genoa, and the Lady
Bianca to finish her letters to the Countess
di Sera and the Lady Vannina.

END OF VOL 1.

T. C. NEWBY, 30, Welbeck Street, Cavendish Square, London.

www.ingramcontent.com/pod-product-compliance
Lightning Source LLC
Chambersburg PA
CBHW021044030726
47496CB00006B/1673